THE
ACCIDENT

Also by Ismail Kadare

The General of the Dead Army
The Wedding
Broken April
The Concert
The Palace of Dreams
The Three-Arched Bridge
The Pyramid
The File on H
Albanian Spring: Anatomy of Tyranny
Elegy for Kosovo
Spring Flowers, Spring Frost

Published by Canongate
The Successor
Chronicle in Stone
Agamemnon's Daughter, with *The Blinding Order*
and *The Great Wall*
The Siege
The Ghost Rider

THE ACCIDENT

A NOVEL

ISMAIL KADARE

TRANSLATED FROM THE
ALBANIAN BY JOHN HODGSON

CANONGATE
Edinburgh · London · New York · Melbourne

Published by Canongate Books in 2010

1

First published in Albanian in 2008 as *Aksidenti* by Onufri Publishing,
Tirana, Albania

First published in Great Britain as *The Accident* in 2010 by
Canongate Books Ltd, 14 High Street, Edinburgh EH1 1TE

www.meetatthegate.com

Recommended by pen

This book has been selected to receive financial assistance from
English PEN's Writers in Translation programme supported by
Bloomberg. English PEN exists to promote literature and its
understanding, uphold writers' freedoms around the world,
campaign against the persecution and imprisonment of writers
for stating their views, and promote the friendly co-operation
of writers and free exchange of ideas.

British Library Cataloguing-in-Publication Data
A catalogue record for this book is available on
request from the British Library

ISBN 978 1 84767 339 8

Typeset in Minion by Palimpsest Book Production Limited,
Falkirk, Stirlingshire

Printed and bound in Great Britain by CPI Mackays, Chatham ME5 8TD

THE
ACCIDENT

Part One

I

It seemed the most ordinary kind of incident. A taxi had veered off the airport autobahn at kilometre marker 17. Its two passengers were killed outright, and the driver, seriously injured, was taken to hospital unconscious.

The police recorded the usual facts in such cases: the names of the victims (a man and a young woman, both Albanian citizens), the registration number of the cab, the name of the Austrian driver and the circumstances, or rather their total ignorance of the circumstances, in which the accident had occurred. There were no signs that the taxi had braked or been hit from any direction. The moving car had slid to the side of the road and somersaulted into a gully, as if the driver had suddenly lost his sight.

A Dutch couple whose car was behind the taxi reported that for no obvious reason the car had suddenly left the carriageway and struck the crash barrier. The terrified pair, if they were not mistaken, had seen the taxi's back doors open as it spun through the air, throwing out the two passengers, a man and a woman.

Another witness, the driver of a Euromobil truck, said more or less the same thing.

A second report, compiled one week later in the hospital after the driver had regained consciousness, only confused the story further. The driver admitted that nothing unusual had happened just before the accident, except that perhaps . . . in the rear-view mirror . . . maybe something had distracted him . . . At this point the policeman lost his patience.

What had he seen in the mirror? The driver could give no answer to the policeman's persistent questioning. The doctor warned him not to tire his patient, but he pressed his point. What was it that he had seen in the mirror above the steering wheel? In other words, what strange thing had happened on the back seat of his cab? Had there been a fight between the two passengers? Or was it the opposite, maybe, a particularly passionate embrace?

The injured driver shook his head. No.

"Then what?" The policeman almost shrieked. "What made you lose your head? What the hell did you see?"

The doctor was about to step in again when the patient resumed his feeble drawl. His reply seemed interminable, and when he finished, the policeman and the doctor stared at each other. The injured driver said that the two passengers on the back seat had done nothing . . . nothing but . . . only . . . they had tried . . . to kiss.

4

2

The driver's evidence was not believed. He was considered to have suffered psychological trauma, and the file on the accident at kilometre marker 17 was closed. The reason for this was simple: whatever the driver's explanation for what he saw or thought he saw in the mirror, it did not change the crux of the matter, that the taxi had overturned as a consequence of something that had happened in his brain, an absence of mind, hallucination or blackout, which it was difficult to believe had had anything to do with his passengers.

As usual, other information surfaced when their names were disclosed. The man, an analyst working for the Council of Europe on western Balkan affairs; the beautiful young woman, an intern at the Archaeological Institute of Vienna. Clearly lovers. The cab had been ordered from the reception of the Miramax Hotel, where the two had stayed for the whole weekend. A technical inspection of the vehicle reported no signs of tampering.

The policeman, in a last effort to flush out any contradictions in the taxi driver's story, asked a trick question. "What happened to the passengers when the car hit the ground?" The driver's reply, that he alone had hit the ground in the car and that the couple were already separated from him in mid-air, showed he was not lying about what he had seen, or thought he had seen.

Although initially routine, the case, because of the taxi driver's strange testimony, was filed away as an "unclassifiable accident".

This was why, several months later, a copy of the file reached the European Road Safety Institute and was passed to the fourth section, which dealt with unusual accidents.

Although the description "unusual" implied that only a handful of such accidents occurred, compared to the common sort caused by bad weather, speeding, exhaustion, drink, drugs and so forth, there was still an astonishing variety of "unclassifiable accidents". The files recorded the most extraordinary incidents, from murderous assaults or vandalised brakes to sudden apparitions that blinded the driver.

Some of them, the most mysterious of all, involved the inside rear-view mirror. These formed a sub-section of their own. Seen in a mirror, only something especially hair-raising could cause an accident. In the case of taxis, the most frequent examples involved passengers threatening the driver with a weapon. There were also many cases of sudden illness: strokes, explosive vomiting of blood, insane fits accompanied by screaming. Sudden fights between passengers, and even knife attacks, were hardly exceptional, but they sometimes distracted inexperienced drivers. Less common were incidents in which one passenger, usually a woman who had climbed into the taxi a few minutes earlier clinging devotedly to her lover, suddenly screamed that she was being abducted and attempted to grab the door handle to leap out. There were even some instances, although they could be counted on the fingers of one hand, in which the driver recognised a passenger as his first love or a wife who had left him.

Explanations were found for most of these initially mysterious cases, but this did not at all mean that everything reflected in rear-view mirrors could be accounted for.

Besides hallucinations, there were cases involving something similar: drivers who were hypnotised by their passenger's eyes, suddenly intoxicated by an enticing glance from a beautiful woman on the back seat or, again the opposite, shaken by a stare from a void that devoured them like a black hole.

What the taxi driver testified to following the accident at kilometre marker 17 on the airport road, although too ordinary to be called a mirage or hallucination, defied all logical explanation. His two passengers' attempt to kiss, which the driver said had caused his confusion and, as a result, both their deaths, was a mystery that deepened the more one struggled to understand it.

The analysts dealing with the accident shook their heads, frowned, smiled cynically and then grew irritated as they went back to the beginning again.

"What does it mean? 'They were trying to kiss.'" It was an unnatural way of putting it, in fact illogical. You could imagine that one of them wanted to kiss the other, while the other refused, or that one of them was nervous, or both were nervous, or that both were scared of a third person, and so on. But it made no sense that two people in a taxi, with only the driver present, were "trying to kiss". *Sie versuchten gerade, sich zu küssen*, as the police report stated. Obvious questions arose. They had just left a hotel where they had spent the night, so why were they "trying to kiss"? In other words, if they wanted to kiss, why didn't they just do it, instead of prevaricating? What was stopping them?

The more you tried to unravel it, the more inextricable it became. Supposing there had been some obstacle between the two passengers which prevented them from coming close – why had this so distracted the driver? Hadn't he carried plenty of passengers who had kissed, or even made love, right there on the back seat? And how had he noticed such a subtle nuance as this attempt to kiss, or rather a desire to kiss, accompanied by an unseen impediment that prevented it?

The frustrated analysts recalled the saying that a fool may throw a stone into a well which a hundred wise men cannot pull out, and noted in the margin that unless it was the old excuse of a driver recognising a passenger as his former wife or lover, which young taxi drivers often produced, having heard it passed down by older colleagues, this must be a genuinely psychotic case and not worth the trouble of dealing with.

Meanwhile, any connection between the driver and the woman in his cab, an Albanian citizen, was ruled out, and a medical report described his psychological condition as entirely normal.

3

Three months later, the archivist could not hide his astonishment when the governments of two Balkan countries, one after another, asked to inspect the file on the accident at kilometre marker 17. How could the states of this quarrelsome peninsula, after committing every possible abomination known to this world – murdering, bombing, setting entire populations at each other's throats and then deporting them – find the time, now that the madness was over, instead of making reparations, to enter into such minor matters as unusual car accidents?

There was no way of knowing why the state of Serbia and Montenegro should take an interest in the accident, but it soon became clear that this country had kept the two victims under surveillance for a long time.

The discovery of this connection was enough to spark the Albanian secret service into action too. Suspicions of a political murder, the kind of allegation fashionable to ridicule, since the fall of communism, as a typical symptom of communist paranoia, suddenly revived in grim earnest.

As usual, the Albanian intelligence officers took a long time to reach a position which the others had already abandoned. However, through contacts with their compatriots in the Albanian communities abroad, they managed to assemble a good deal of material relating to the victims. There were parts of letters, photographs, airline tickets, hotel addresses and bills, which, although only the first fruits of their harvest, provided a mass of information about the couple. The photographs, taken mainly in hotels, at pavement cafés, and a few in a bath, out of which the young woman, naked, stared at the camera with more elation than shame, left the nature of their relationship in no doubt. The hotel bills were clear evidence that they had met in different European cities, where this woman's friend had happened to go for his work: Strasbourg, Vienna, Rome, Luxembourg.

The photographs confirmed the locations, and the cities were also mentioned in letters, mainly written by the young woman, who liked deciding in which of them she had felt happiest.

The intelligence officers placed their main hope of solving the riddle in these letters, but after reading them they were at first disappointed, then disoriented and finally totally bewildered.

The blatant contradictions led them to interrupt their investigations to interview hotel receptionists, chambermaids, waiters in late-night bars, a girlfriend of the woman, called Shpresa, an Albanian living in Switzerland who the letters stated "knew the truth" and, finally, the taxi driver.

Their testimonies more or less coincided: usually when they met, the couple seemed cheerful, but on occasion the woman had appeared despondent, and once had been seen silently weeping while he had gone out to make a phone call. He too had sometimes looked sad, and then she would try to comfort him, stroking and kissing his hand.

The interviewers put the question: was something on their minds . . . a decision they had to take but couldn't, some regret, uncertainty, threat? The waiters could not answer this. To their eyes it all seemed normal. Most couples in late-night bars passed from ebullience to silence, and sometimes dejection, and then suddenly brightened up again.

The woman became very beautiful at these times. Her eyes, which until then had idly followed her cigarette smoke, lit up with emotion. Her cheeks too. She acquired an alarming, devastating charm.

Devastating? What could that mean?

"I don't know how to explain it. I was trying to say the kind of beauty that knocks you flat, as people say. The man also seemed to revive, and would order another whisky. Then they would talk again in their own language until after midnight, and stand up to go upstairs to their room.

"From the way she rose to her feet with a sidelong glance and walked in front with her head slightly bowed, an old-fashioned picture of a beautiful, transgressing woman, you could tell that they were going to make love. These things provide late-night barmen with entertainment, especially at the end of their long hotel shifts."

4

None of the other information, gathered in various places, helped the intelligence officers to pin down the facts at all. In the wake of the waiters' evidence, the dead couple's letters seemed even less coherent. Sometimes they read like the ordinary correspondence of lovers, even when she complained of his behaviour. Yet sometimes their tone was entirely different, and the terse notes between them suggested that this was a purely routine relationship between a call girl and her client.

The officers could hardly believe their eyes when they read phrases of hers such as "Whatever happens, I will love you all my life," followed by notes from him on later dates, giving his hotel address and adding, "Everything OK on the same terms as last time?"

This could be interpreted in two ways. He could be referring to the length of their stay – one, two or more nights – but it rather hinted at remuneration. Moreover, now and then the expression "call girl" appeared, and he seemed eager to use it, whether accurately or not.

In her earlier letters she would quote phrases of his that implied he had once written quite normally – about how he had missed her, was impatient to see her, and so forth. The change apparently took place during the final phase of their long association.

Careful calculation revealed that their relationship had lasted some twelve years, and that their estrangement had occurred only in the last fifty-two weeks. The expression "call girl", like some boundary marker, appeared forty weeks before their deaths.

"I admit that you have given me boundless happiness," she had written in one of her letters, "but just as often your cruel irritability has made my life a misery."

She had continually complained of this, and in a letter dated 2000 told him that the only time she had felt totally happy with him had been during the year of the Kosovo War, when he seemed to discharge his nervous tension in an entirely different direction.

"After Serbia was defeated you didn't seem to know what to do with yourself and you turned on me again."

This final phrase led the Albanian intelligence officers to believe that they had solved one of the mysteries: the reason for Besfort Y.'s surveillance by the Serbian and Montenegrin secret service. With his many contacts in Strasbourg and Brussels, and inside most of the international human rights organisations, Besfort Y. was naturally the kind of person to be a thorn in the side of Yugoslavia, and might in a way be deemed responsible for its bombing.

It was easy to deduce why this surveillance began at such a late stage, after the war was over. Just at this time, a kind of remorse at the punishment and dismemberment of Yugoslavia led to attempts to revise the facts. Thousands of people were either elated or thrown into despair at the prospect of the bombing being called a mistake.

As the tide of this campaign swelled, it became normal to sling mud at people like Besfort Y. and all those who had worked for the demise of Yugoslavia. His girlfriend's letter could be interpreted to show that this man, driven by a kind of perverse fury, would not rest in peace until this neighbouring state was crushed, and that his girlfriend, perhaps his inspiration, was just an ordinary hooker.

Reluctant though they were to admit it, the Albanian intelligence officers suspected that there was an element of truth in what the Serbs said, especially about Besfort Y.'s girlfriend. In an attempt to prove the opposite, the interviewers did their rounds again, visiting the travel agencies, bars, hotel swimming pools and the small apartment where some of the dead woman's cardboard boxes were still in the cellar.

This did nothing to dispel the confusion in their minds. They began to genuinely suspect that there had been not one but two women whose identities they had mixed up.

Or so they would have liked to believe, but to their despair they became more and more convinced that this young woman of such disturbing loveliness, whom they now knew so well from her letters, the testimonies of others and especially from private photographs, merely concealed within herself a second nature.

5

The appearance on the scene of the pianist Liza Blumberg, Rovena's friend, revived the suspicion of murder.

Any involvement of the Serbian secret service had been ruled out at an early stage. Conceivably, Besfort Y. had been eliminated as someone damaging to Yugoslavia, and with him his girlfriend, who happened to be present at the fatal moment. But it was against all logic for this to happen at such a late date. Besfort Y.'s disappearance would have been useful at the proper time but it served no one's purpose now that the war was over.

The rewriting of events required Besfort Y. not to be killed but discredited. His death would not do this, and would even make it more difficult. It is a known fact that it is easier to defame the living than the dead. Besfort Y. could be no exception, still less his girlfriend.

What was new and surprising in the evidence of Lulu Blumb, as the pianist was known to her circle of friends, was that she linked Rovena's death not to the Serbian secret service but to her partner. She said that recently there had been a tendency to disguise murders as mishaps, and she firmly believed that Besfort Y. had been determined to get rid of his girlfriend by means of an accident, even if he himself shared her fate.

At this point every interviewer interrupted the pianist and, with unconcealed sarcasm, said that it was hard to accuse one of these two of murdering the other when they had somersaulted into the gully together, unless one imagined that Besfort Y., as they fell, had seized this moment of confusion to commit the crime!

"Wait, don't laugh too soon," said Lulu Blumb. "I'm not so crazy as to think that." Then she put forward her own version.

She was convinced that Besfort Y. had killed his girlfriend. Rovena herself had told her that a few months previously, when they were in Albania and B.Y. had taken her to a shady motel, she had been frightened for her life. Lulu preferred not to go into the reasons why. The intelligence officers were in a better position to discover these. She was a pianist and knew nothing about the dark underside of politics. Besfort Y. had been a complex person. Rovena had once told Lulu about some mysterious phone calls that had come in the small hours. They were about some quarrel with Israel, or over Israel, she couldn't quite remember. As she said, she had no wish to be involved in arguments of this kind. Even if she had been opposed to the bombing of Yugoslavia, this was not out of firm political conviction but simply a general aversion to war. Meanwhile, the discovery of the nature of the relationship between Rovena and the pianist damaged the latter's credibility. It was not hard to see, and indeed Lulu herself did not hide it, that the two had been involved in a lengthy affair, which naturally made the pianist jealous of Besfort Y.

This was the reason why, even after Blumberg's intervention, the investigators paid little heed to her surmises, and especially not to the later episode, the most bewildering of all, in which the pianist first mentioned a large doll torn apart by dogs and then told them not to take any notice of what she said, because she was tired. The interviewers of course came back to the doll, but the pianist said that she had read about it in reports of the deaths, that she was really very tired, and that the only thing she could tell them was that she was sure it had not been Rovena St. but a totally different woman in the cab.

Most reports underlined this last phrase, but the interviewers would have refused to believe her and might not have come back to this point, or even to the suspicion of murder in general, if they had not stumbled upon other evidence – this time from "his" side.

This testimony, apparently the only one of its kind, came from an old college friend of Besfort Y., with whom he had had a conversation on the first floor of the Davidoff Bar in Tirana, one autumn day, a few months before his death.

According to the witness, Besfort had been in a sombre mood. Asked what the matter was, he at first answered vaguely. He had problems. Later he came back of his own accord to his incomplete reply. He had got badly mixed up . . . with a young woman.

Knowing the sort of man he was, the witness had not asked

any more questions. Besfort, unusually for him, volunteered a little more. He thought he had made a mistake. The witness had the impression that Besfort considered any relationship with this woman to be a mistake. To his surprise, he used the word "fear", though whether he was scared of the relationship or of the woman herself, the witness could not tell.

After a long silence, he repeated that he had gone wrong somewhere. He offered no further explanation, but said that he would try to get out of this mess. He could do it. He became less and less coherent. He believed that when the time came – that is, at the right moment – he would know what to do.

The tone of his conversation brooked no interruption. Facial expression? Manner? Cold. "Oh no, not like a murderer at all. I would just say cold. Pitiless."

The interviewers went back to the suspicions of Liza Blumb, and even to her almost delirious words about a doll found in the bushes, torn by dogs, but the pianist, erratic as ever, or stricken by remorse at having talked so much, refused to cooperate further.

This did not stop the inquiry proceeding. In fact, now that the pianist was out of the picture, the intelligence officers unexpectedly became all the more keen. Not often had a suspicion of murder led them to examine such minute details to the point that they would forget what they were looking for.

The analysts sifted through all the information, including the new material gathered during the latest research, with a dedication beyond the call of duty.

They returned to the first two statements given by the Dutch couple and the driver of the Euromobil truck. Initially they seemed to agree (the taxi's open doors, the bodies thrown out), but a careful examination showed this not to be the case. According to the couple, the bodies of the victims were still together as they fell through the air, their arms round each other's necks, as if trying to hold tight to one another. But the truck driver insisted that the bodies were apart as they fell.

But the evidence of Rovena's friend Shpresa in Switzerland, who recalled cryptic remarks on the phone, also pointed towards murder.

Yet this explanation was hardly tenable. Other stubborn facts, mysterious scattered phrases and cryptic remarks on the phone, according to the evidence of Rovena's friend in Switzerland, roused suspicions of another kind.

In a letter written less than a year previously, Rovena had said, "You seem so calm now. I preferred your old irritability, that short temper which brought me such unhappiness, to this terrifying reticence."

In another note, apparently written quite some time afterwards, she recalled a phone call of the previous evening: "What you said to me last night may have been superficially kind, but was essentially, I don't know how to put it, frightening, destructive, as cold as outer space."

At about the same time she admitted to Shpresa that she was extremely unhappy.

"Because of 'him'?" asked her friend.

"Yes," she said, "but I can't tell you on the phone. It's very hard to explain. Perhaps impossible. I'll try when we meet."

But they never met again, and two months later the accident happened.

Asked by the intelligence officers whether she nevertheless had any particular suspicions, Shpresa replied only after a long silence. Of course she had partly worked it out, if only vaguely. "I've got problems with Besfort," Rovena had said on several other occasions, just generally, as anybody might open a conversation of this kind. When asked what sort of problems, she had replied that they were not easy to explain, and added after a silence: "B. is trying to persuade me we don't need each other any more."

"What sort of talk is that?" Shpresa had asked. When Rovena said nothing, her friend persisted. "And so? Does he want you to split up?"

"No," the other woman had said.

"Then I don't understand. What does he want?"

"Something else," she had replied, taking a different tack.

"I don't understand you," her friend said. "I haven't understood you for a long time. That friend of yours has always been beyond me, but now you are too."

"Perhaps this is something to talk about when we meet again," Rovena responded, "like we did a few weeks ago."

The officers were able to connect the victim's diary notes and various phrases jotted down for future letters to this enigmatic conversation between the two women.

"Hope of resurrection?" she noted on a piece of paper with no date. "You are pretending to give me hope that you will again be the person you once were. You write that everything that rises again must first die, as if this were some sort of reassurance. But it just leads me deeper into darkness."

On the telephone pad, three months before the accident, she had written alongside the address of a hotel: "Our first meeting . . . after the void. Strange! He seems to have infected me with his own madness."

The intelligence officers could not make anything of this.

One week before the accident, there was a similar note in her pocket diary: "Friday, Miramax Hotel, our third *post-mortem* meeting."

As if to cling to something tangible and concrete, the officers kept reverting to the last evening in the late-night bar of the Miramax Hotel, reconstructing it hour by hour on the evidence given by the waiters. Their huddled conversation in the dim corner. Her loosened hair. They left after midnight, but he returned after an hour, with that expression of exhausted quiescence worn by men who come back down to the bar after making love, giving their partners time to rest alone.

Then, at quite a different tempo, there came the glass of Irish whisky, morning, the order for the taxi and the driver's cruelly stilted phrase: *Sie versuchten gerade, sich zu küssen.*

6

Everywhere in the world events flow noisily on the surface, while their deep currents pull silently, but nowhere is this contrast so striking as in the Balkans.

Gales sweep the mountains, lashing the tall firs and mighty oaks, and the whole peninsula appears demented.

Yet what happens deep below in the world of rumours and undercover investigations may also be taken for madness, often of an even more serious kind.

Or that is what an external observer might have thought of the two secret services as they zealously followed the trail of this case, which was becoming more like a ghost story.

It was the Serbian agents who showed the first signs of flagging. Their Albanian counterparts, although reluctant to admit it, felt that they had become entangled in this case simply in order not to fall behind their rivals, and could hardly wait to give it up.

It was some time later, when least expected, that a researcher's careful hand delved once again into the deep recesses of the archives. The delicacy of this hand with its long, thin, elegant fingers drew attention to the many marks left on the arm by anxious nurses struggling to find a vein to take blood. The researcher unearthed not only the files of the two victims but also hundreds of other statements by witnesses, known and unknown. And so, month by month and year by year, an astonishingly variegated mosaic took shape. Where the secret services of two states had failed, this single researcher almost succeeded in solving the riddle of kilometre marker 17. He did this without funds or resources or powers of constraint, indeed without any motivation of duty or profit, but solely under the pressure of a personal concern never revealed to anybody.

Just as a galaxy may, from a distance, appear immobile, but to a close observer reveals the terrible convulsions and explosions of light roaring in its depths, so the file of this researcher, whose name was never divulged, displayed, apparently at random, but in fact in an esoteric order, the myriad tiny fragments making up the mosaic. Of course, all the old data was there, mostly enriched with new details. There were the names of hotels, even the numbers of the rooms in which the couple had slept, the evidence of cleaners and barmen. There were bills of all kinds, charges for phone calls, fitness centres, driving lessons, visits to the doctor and prescription receipts. This was not all. There were Besfort Y.'s two dreams, told directly to Rovena, one with a transparent meaning and the other totally impenetrable. Again there were fragments of letters, diaries, subsequent recon-structions of phone conversations, mostly accompanied by suppositions and deductions that at first seemed contradictory but could later be reconciled, only to diverge and merge again in ever more startling ways.

The woman had grouped together days of happiness with a precision that recalled the weather reports on the evening news, comparing one hotel to another, the intensity of pleasure and the degree of excitement. All these notes were matched to the testimonies of the female staff, who remembered the kind of perfume the young woman wore, the lingerie carelessly discarded at the foot of the bed and the stains on the sheets showing that the couple never took precautions. Equally precise were her records of hours of despondency after angry phone conversations, her complaints and her despair. Between these two states there was a third, perhaps harder to describe, a grey zone, as if shrouded in mist.

She used this very word "zone" in one of the rare letters she had sent to Shpresa in Switzerland.

"Our meetings are now in a new zone. It's no exaggeration to say a different planet. Ruled by different laws. It has a chilly quality, frightening of course, but still I must admit that it has its strange and attractive side . . . I know that this will surprise you, but I hope to explain when we meet."

"But as you know we never saw each other again," said her correspondent.

Another letter, still less coherent, was written two weeks before the accident.

"I feel numb again. He still exerts a hypnotic power over me. The things that at first seemed the most ridiculous to me are now the ones I accept most easily. Last night he said that all this confusion and misunderstanding between us recently was caused by the soul. Now that we have put that aside, we might say we have been saved. It is easier to understand each other through the body. I'm sure you'll think I'm crazy. I thought so at first. But not later. Anyway, we'll meet soon and you will see then that I'm right."

The researcher worked patiently through this maze for hours on end. It was the soul that caused misunderstanding. The meeting before their death, called *post-mortem*. Other abstruse phrases. Each one of them in turn seemed the key to unlocking the truth, or sometimes the key that shut it away for ever.

It was this very meeting, just before their deaths, that was called *post*. Apart from this extraordinary paradox, the final letter or note written by Besfort Y. and found in the young woman's handbag on the day of the accident, which began disconcertingly with the words, "OK on the same terms as last time?" and was the very message that had prompted the secret services to step up their investigations into him, related to this same last meeting at the Miramax Hotel.

There was a cryptic phone conversation with her friend in Switzerland, which Shpresa had not wanted to talk about at all. She was persuaded to do so after reading what the reports called the "cynical note", which gave this phone call an intelligible meaning.

"You say I shouldn't worry. You tell me these things are unimportant compared to the happiness he brings me. But if I tell you he treats me almost like a prostitute?"

"He dares to treat you like a prostitute? Do you understand what this means? What am I supposed to make of it?"

"Of course I know what this means. I'll say it again. He uses the phrase 'call girl', not prostitute, but that's how he treats me, like a whore."

"And you put up with this?"

". . . Yes . . ."

"This is beyond me, and to tell the truth you're driving me crazy more than he is."

"You're right. But you don't understand the whole truth. Perhaps it's my fault for trying to explain on the phone. I hope, when we meet . . ."

"Listen, Rovena. It's not hard to understand that if he treats you like a whore, he has his reasons. He wants to humiliate you in every way he can."

"Of course he does, but still . . ."

"No buts. Humiliation is humiliation."

"I was trying to say, perhaps it's more complicated than that. Do you remember that film we talked about, *La Dame aux Camélias*? Where that character genuinely loves the woman but, in a flash of anger, to insult her, he leaves a wad of banknotes under her pillow?"

"Has he gone that far?"

"No . . . but wait . . . this is the sort of thing that happens in love."

"Rovena, you're talking nonsense. People in love have quarrels and lose their temper. But as far as I can gather, he does this on purpose, deliberately."

"It's true. That's how he behaves. Why?"

"Why? That's exactly what I can't make out. Perhaps he resents you in some way. He wants to get his own back. Perhaps . . . I don't know what to say."

"No, he's not that sort of person. Unlike me. Sometimes I can barely control myself. But he's not like that."

"He wants to degrade you. He wants to crush you, destroy you morally. Not to say physically . . . Don't you see?"

"But why? Why should he need to do that?"

"He alone knows. You told me you're frightened of him. Perhaps he's frightened of you."

"Frightened of what?"

"I don't know. You're both frightened of each other. Not just frightened but scared witless . . . never mind. Rovena, darling, think hard about this business. I don't want you to worry, but look after yourself! I have an uncanny feeling . . ."

7

It was hard to tell which results of the inquiry the secret services had found useful in building up their portrait of Besfort Y. Sometimes it may have been the names of the hotels, especially when these hotels, or the cities where they were located, were also mentioned in the files on "Albanian terrorists", as the Yugoslavs called the insurgent leaders when they travelled to these places. However, they had also probably relied on the more ingenious interpretations of Besfort's behaviour as "psychotic", based mainly on the evidence of Rovena St.'s conversations with her friends. To one friend, Rovena had recounted Besfort's dreams of a summons to The Hague. Then there were Shpresa's parting words on the phone: "look after yourself! I have an uncanny feeling . . ."

Meanwhile, Besfort Y.'s final message, now known as the "cynical note", was translated into most of the working languages of the Council of Europe, sometimes with cautious annotations: "Is this translation accurate? Do the words 'conditions' and 'OK' have the same connotations in the Albanian original?" These were quoted alongside the Serbian commentaries which were eager to show that the analyst Besfort Y. was a dangerous schizophrenic, or worse.

On the list of twenty-nine personalities whose comments and reporting, according to the Serbian intelligence services, had succeeded in bamboozling the governments of the West, Besfort Y. was a lesser light when set against stars of the first magnitude such as Bill Clinton, Wesley Clark, Madeleine Albright and the rest. However, when it came to obscure impulses, often of a personal origin, which had turned these leading figures against poor Yugoslavia, then Besfort Y. was the only one whose commitment could be compared to that of the American president. The latter's affair with Monica Lewinsky was like a harmless idyll when set against the poisonous fury of this Albanian analyst, to whom destroying a state seemed to offer the same satisfaction as possessing, or rather subjugating, a woman. The reported phrase "after Serbia was defeated, you turned on me again" left no doubt that this analyst's political passions had affected his love life.

The unidentified researcher explained more lucidly than any of his predecessors why the secret services became even more keen after the drama was over. It was true that the curtain had fallen and the Hague Tribunal now had the former Serbian leader on trial, but there was no stemming the flood of Europe's remorse. The entire conflict was being reassessed, and shouts of "Send them to The Hague!" grew ever more strident, and this time not for the vanquished, but for the victors. As one historian wrote, Serbia hoped to recover her lost Kosovo not by force of arms but with the help of pathos and pity for her ruin.

As if compensating for the obscure and enigmatic parts, this section of the inquiry was of exemplary clarity, with endless names, dates, newspaper headlines, quotations from the news, statements and rebuttals. Personalities with totally contrary opinions jostled together. Alain Ducelier, William Walker, Tony Blair, Günter Grass, Noam Chomsky, André Glucksmann, Harold Pinter, Bernard-Henri Lévy, Paul Garde, Peter Handke, Pascal Bruckner, Mother Teresa, Ibrahim Dominik Rugova, Seamus Heaney, Pope John Paul II, Patrick Besson, Gabriel Keller, Ismail Kadare, Claude Durand, Bernard Kouchner, Régis Debray, Jacques Chirac Pontifex (defender of the bridges of Belgrade), Bogdan Bogdanović Ponticrash (architect and ideologist of the destruction of these same bridges), the Dalai Lama, Cardinal Ratzinger, and so on.

According to the unnamed researcher, both the Serbs' gratitude to their defenders and their hatred for their destroyers, which Balkan custom suggested would persist for centuries, had unexpectedly begun to fade. The new geopolitics of the peninsula, the Stability Pact for South Eastern Europe and the queue at the gates of Europe as these stubborn states, whether allies or enemies yesterday, waited together to join the family of their dreams, had achieved the impossible. Their vows of revenge, their rage and whining of the past were now recalled with more curiosity than pain.

Certain rumours at the time were slower to fade, such as

the persistent claim that Mother Teresa had been the moving spirit behind the bombing of Yugoslavia, with her midnight phone call to the American president, "My son, do something for my Albanians, punish Serbia," while a song about the punitive president went round the bars:

> Take Monica away
> And the Serbs will pay.
> If you miss getting laid
> Give it to Belgrade . . .

Now the researcher himself, always detached and impartial, suddenly seemed to be in a hurry to set aside this epic conclusion of events, and to follow an entirely different track.

8

The inquiry now resembled a plane which, after flying across a clear sky, re-enters a patch of turbulence. Dark surmises, grave suspicions, ambiguous phrases, obscure scraps of dialogue drawn from half-remembered phone conversations loomed out of the fog and vanished again. Besfort had written: "In your last letter you mentioned defeating me. Did you really dream of such a thing, even for a moment? Don't you realise that I might be more dangerous in defeat?" Her reply: "Believe me, this misunderstanding between us has worn me down." His answer: "Don't worry about a thing like that. This sort of anxiety comes from the body, not the soul."

Then Rovena talked to her friend Shpresa.

"He told me yesterday that I should keep to the pact between us."

"What pact? This is the first time you've mentioned such a thing."

"Really?"

"If I'm really your friend, you must be more honest."

"I know, but do you think this is easy for me?"

"This story just gets more obscure."

"Have you heard of Empedocles?"

"Hm, I think I've heard the name, but I'm not sure."

"He was new to me too. He's an ancient philosopher. Out of curiosity to see what no human eye had seen before, he threw himself into the crater of Etna."

"So? What's he got to do with you?"

"Not me, the two of us."

"I still don't understand."

"Well, one day he said to me that we would try something totally unfamiliar, and he mentioned this famous man Empedocles."

"Rovena, I don't understand you. Are you going to throw yourself off a cliff because some crazy character did so five thousand years ago?"

"Slow down. I'm not as far gone as that. It was just a comparison. What we were taught at school to call a metaphor. But still, just imagining it makes me scared."

"Of course it's scary. Just your talking about it makes my skin crawl. Someone jumping into the lava out of curiosity . . . a funny sort of curiosity!"

"Is that how you imagined the crater? Active?"

"What?"

"I was asking if you imagined the crater with molten lava or not?"

"Is that important? When you mentioned a volcano, I thought of lava."

"But I imagined it extinct, black, desolate. And like that it's twice as frightening. Wait, he said that this was what falling into a black hole would be like, coming out into another dimension . . ."

"Listen, Rova, and don't misunderstand me. It would be good if you came here as soon as you can. Take a few days' rest. This Alpine air will do you good. We'll have a good time together, like in the old days. We'll remember all those jokes from university. Remember that doggerel by the guy from Durrës in the other seminar group?

Rova is an antibiotic
Short for Rovamycin
But Rovena is hypnotic
Elegant and enticing.

The researcher used the young woman's words "I'm scared", repeated over and over again, as the starting point for his questioning of the taxi driver.

"She said, 'I'm scared, but I don't know why. I pretend not to be frightened of him. He also pretends not to frighten me any more. But none of this is true.' Why were you so shaken by what you saw, or thought you saw, in the mirror?"

This question, although lifted from the written record, had lost none of its ominous weight.

"Did it remind you of anything? Even dimly, or indirectly? Some kind of obstacle, a taboo, something that should never happen?"

"I don't know what to say. I'm not sure."

"Were you scared?"

"Yes."

Everybody in this story was scared, with or without reason. They were scared of one other, of themselves or of someone, no one could tell who.

Some part of this fear had been conveyed through the mirror in the taxi. But where had the rest come from?

The researcher finally succeeded in meeting Lulu Blumb, getting her to talk and ensuring her continued cooperation. Her suspicion of murder was difficult to dismiss, but also hard to confirm.

She almost exploded with rage. "Are you blind, or just pretending? You could tell a mile off that he was the murderous kind. That dream of his, or rather his nightmare, about the Hague Tribunal showed that."

The researcher wanted to butt in to say that these days a lot of people were scared of The Hague – Serbs, Croats, Albanians, Montenegrins. You might say that the whole Balkans went in fear and trembling. But he restrained himself.

Lulu Blumb went on to say that neither the dream about the court summons nor the second one, which people generally called inexplicable, enigmatic and so forth, held any mystery for her. She said that the researcher no doubt knew about the funereal building, a cross between a mausoleum and a motel, at which a person knocks and looks for someone, who later turns out to be a young woman who is locked inside, turned to stone or murdered by some means.

The inquiry stated that Besfort Y. had had this dream one

week before his death. Logically, he should have had this dream later, after killing Rovena. But as the researcher might be aware (and might well know better than she did) such displacements are quite common in dreams. The dream showed most of all that Besfort had already resolved to kill Rovena.

The researcher listened to the pianist with the same calm curiosity, both when he believed her and when he didn't. This woman had a special talent, perhaps granted to her by music, for evoking the atmosphere of events, especially imagined events. For instance, whenever she described the final dream, she never forgot to mention the building's midnight glow, which was a reflection of the plaster, or perhaps of despair.

Her description of the other incident on the morning of 17 May caused in the researcher's mind an intoxicating frisson, whenever she mentioned it, that he could never shake off.

Dozens, hundreds of times, he imagined Besfort Y. walking through the rain and mist, holding the shape of a woman tight against himself – whether real or not, nobody knew.

As if ensnared by this scene, he was scarcely able to move on to ask, "So what happened later, in your opinion?"

Lulu Blumb, also caught in her own trap, seemed unwilling to answer. As he silently rehearsed the questions to himself, he thought he saw her scowl even before he spoke. "Who knows what happened next," she said aloud. Tell me what happened next, Miss Blumb, he said to himself. "We know that she was accompanying him to the airport, but did not plan to travel herself. So we know that everything that could possibly have happened took place in the taxi between the hotel and the airport terminal. In fact something did happen, but it involved the entire taxi and all of the people inside. It is like imagining, at a time when two countries are at war, some catastrophe striking the entire planet . . . perhaps you think imagining a murder is the same as committing one. Sometimes that is how it seems to me. But this time we are trying to work out the murderer's plan, even though it was not carried out by him, but by some external force. The possibilities of such a thing happening after they left the hotel are limited. Only if they stopped somewhere along the road, at some small building or secluded place . . . 'Driver, please stop here. We have to do something at that chapel over there . . .'"

Lulu Blumb sighed, implying that they were thinking on entirely different lines and would never agree on anything.

"But you can still tell me the motive for the murder," the researcher said aloud, certain that she would merely fold her arms.

The pianist did not get angry, but suddenly drew close to him and said gently that she had wanted to talk about this for a long time, but nobody would listen to her. She had talked about the late-night phone calls, about the Shin Bet, the Israeli secret service, and his terror of the Hague Tribunal. But the investigators did not want to know. Obviously they were scared. Besfort Y. had been a danger to anyone who came near him. Especially to a woman who had slept with him. Apparently he had talked to her about things he should never have mentioned, and had later regretted it.

"Everybody knows what happens when a violent person has second thoughts: the witness disappears. Rovena St. knew the most appalling things. Any one of them would make your hair stand on end. I can tell you, for example, that she knew the precise hour when Yugoslavia would be bombed, two days in advance. You see why I don't want to talk about these things?"

The inquiry dragged on and grew, sending out new tendrils in all kinds of directions. The researcher made visible efforts to dispel the fog, but equally obvious were his attempts to hide behind it.

Finally, towards the middle of the file, the question arose of why these two protagonists, Besfort Y. and Rovena St., seemed to be trying to cover up their love for each other by pretending to be whore and client.

Delving deeper, the researcher wondered whether Besfort Y. and his friend were merely two people outside the normal order of things.

It was in this part of the file that the researcher for the first time drew attention to his own self, like a man who wanders along an uncertain path and takes care to leave behind certain tokens of recognition, pebbles or dropped ash. After the words "But who am I, trying to enter where no one can go?" there came another phrase: "Look for me and you will find me!"

Apparently certain that another researcher would follow in his footsteps, and another after that, because the lust for knowledge is as inexhaustible and cyclic as the waves of the ocean of humanity, the author of the inquiry addressed his future counterpart. His words, the more one studied them, resembled the lament of someone who has fallen by his own fault into a trap or a deep dungeon and begs for rescue.

9

In an appendix to the first part of the inquiry, the researcher returned to what he called the "intrinsic perversity" of the entire story.

It wasn't merely the speech, the phrases in the conversations and notes that sounded stilted, in other words it was not just that the linguistic style had stiffened, as if under a sudden blow or toxic attack, but that its inner logic appeared disjointed. Rephrasing the content and turning it into normal language still revealed traces of the unnatural, which showed that the flaw lay deeper, and was more essential.

The researcher spent years trying to reach the heart of the matter, like a workman going underground to find damaged cables.

His notes revealed his own agony as much as the suffering of the vanished couple, in a distorting perspective that was at times as intoxicating and liberating as a new vision of the world, and sometimes totally disabling.

What led the two lovers so willingly into such perverseness?

The death of love is like an enveloping chill. But it is never experienced equally by both partners. There is always one on whom the burden of suffering weighs most, at least at first.

However, this was something totally different. The question might be put in another way: were both of them, or only one, to be considered as *post mortem*?

It had to be only one of them. One of them had struck a blow at the other. But which?

Again and again the researcher came back to the same question. What had made this couple experience as normal a situation that seemed totally out of this world? What did they know, what did they see that others could not? What hidden laws had they uncovered, what different sequence or flow of time? He was so close. He needed only one step to carry him across into a new dimension of thought. But this single step was impossible.

What was this chain that tethered his mind, like a wild beast, within certain bounds? The suspicion dogged him that these two had been able, if only for an instant, to unleash this animal. They had stepped over the bounds and been lost.

He sometimes thought that what had happened related to the familiar doubt as to whether love really exists, or is merely a sick, over-the-rainbow fantasy, a new phantasm that has appeared on our planet only in the last five or six thousand years. Perhaps we still can't tell if our planet will accept it, or reject it as foreign tissue.

Whistle-blowers had sounded the alarm about the hole in

the ozone layer, about the encroaching deserts, and terrorism, but nobody had yet drawn attention to the fragile state of love. Perhaps a few sects had been created to investigate the truth or falseness of love, and maybe this couple, Besfort Y. and Rovena St., had been members of one of these.

One starry summer night, he felt that he was closer than ever to the forbidden zone, but on its very brink he had collapsed, as if struck by an epileptic fit.

He spent the entire summer in a lethargic depression of the kind that can land you in hospital.

Determined to keep going in spite of every danger, he thought he would try a new approach, using his research data to reconstruct, day by day and month by month, the story of what might have passed on earth between Rovena St. and Besfort Y. during the last forty weeks of their lives. Like Plato, he knew that this story could only be a pale reflection of its eternal form, yet he clung to the hope of finding the essence by starting from the appearance, however misleading this might be.

It would not be an easy task to tell the story of their last forty weeks, and maybe it would turn out to be impossible. The torrent of events surged ahead, and could not be controlled.

Perhaps he could tame it if he divided it into days and months, or acts or cantos, like an ancient epic.

He had heard that *The Iliad* took four days to tell. Would this be enough for his story too? Like every story, it would have three phases: the first purely imagined, the second clothed in words and the third finally told to others.

He had a presentiment that he would only be able to manage the first.

And so, one night in late summer, he started to imagine their story. But this effort of imagination was so strenuous, and consumed so much passion and empathy, that it drained his entire life-blood away.

Part Two

Chapter One

Forty weeks before. A hotel. Morning.

As so often in hotels, wakefulness crept up on him from the window. He stared at the curtains for a moment, trying to work out from them which hotel he was in. They told him nothing, not even the city. But he could still recall precisely his dream of a few moments before.

He turned his head. Rovena's hair, spilt over the pillow, made her face and bare shoulder look even more fragile than usual.

Besfort Y. had always thought that women's smooth necks and graceful arms were the sort of things that could be used as tactical weapons in war, as decoys by opposing armies.

Fragile, as if he could break her in his arms and master her easily: that is how Rovena had looked twelve years ago, when, for the first time, she had come out of the bath to lie beside him and conquer him. Her breasts were small, like a teenager's, and strategically important in the battle. After them came her belly, the next snare. Below this, dark, threatening, marked by the dark triangle, lurked the final hurdle. And here he was defeated.

Carefully, so as not to wake her, he lifted the quilt and, as he had done dozens of times before, looked at her belly and the site of his surrender. It was surely the only place in the world where happiness could be found only in defeat.

He covered her up again with the same gentleness and looked at his watch. It was nearly time for her to wake up. Perhaps he still had time to tell her his dream before it faded irretrievably.

How many times, he said to himself, had they repeated all this in one hotel or another, without being entirely sure what "all this" was.

In his dream he had been eating lunch with Stalin. This seemed entirely normal, and it even made no particular impression on him when Stalin's face alternated with that of a high-school classmate, a certain Thanas Rexha.

"My right hand has gone numb. It's been like this for four days," Stalin said to him. "You sign these two treaties for me."

While he was signing the first treaty, he wanted to ask what it was about. But the second was quickly put in front of him. "It's secret, but take a look at it if you like." He felt no eagerness to read the text, but still, more out of a desire to please than out of curiosity, he glanced through the second treaty. It was extremely complicated, with knotty passages that apparently contradicted each other. He remembered again Thanas Rexha, who had given up high school after twice failing the history exam about the German–Soviet Nonaggression Pact on the eve of World War II.

What a crazy dream, he thought. It had continued, but he could not remember how. His eyes wandered from the curtains back to Rovena's face. Her eyelids were still closed in sleep, but fluttered slightly like a swallow in distress. Normally he got up before her, and whenever he studied her sleeping face, he thought that a woman who is loved opens her eyes in a different way to others.

But Rovena did not wake, and he got up and went to the window in the anteroom, a long way from the bed. He drew aside the curtain slightly and looked stonily at the street, where yellow leaves were falling.

Abstractedly, he listed the names of hotels where they had slept: Plaza, Intercontinental, Palace, Don Pepe, Sacher, Marriott. Their lights glittered palely, blue, orange, crimson. Why was he calling these hotels to mind as if looking for help? And why did they hurry past?

He felt a chill round his shoulders and turned to enter the bathroom. That same soft light glowed below the mirror. It came from her toiletries, her perfume, comb, creams, which had no doubt acquired something special over the years from contact with her face.

Among their sweetest moments had been the times when she had sat on the little white throne next to the bath and washed herself. Under the surface of the water, the patch of her bush would continually change shape, grow fuzzy, ambiguous.

"What are you thinking about?" she would ask him, lifting her eyes from her own body to look at him. "Will you go out for a bit while I get ready?"

He would lie on the bed waiting, and listen as she sang familiar tunes softly to herself.

The night before, they had repeated this ritual almost exactly. But this had not prevented him from thinking again what he had said to her on the street: "Something is not the same as before."

Rovena was still asleep when he emerged from the shower, without even that clear expression on her face that generally preceded her awakening. Her cheeks and forehead were dull. He remembered when she first arrived, years before. She had sat down, after a sleepless night, as she explained to him later, with the glitter that was fashionable at the time clinging to her cheeks, like the crumbs of dreams. She had looked him straight in the eye to tell him what she had been thinking about on the way: the words of a French song, *J'ai tant rêvé de toi.*

He had never heard such a natural and direct declaration of love.

I will love you all my life. Yours desperately. He had attached words to that first meeting, like the glitter on her cheeks, that he knew had not been spoken or written until later.

Again, as if looking for help, he thought of the late-night bars with their tiny lights and resonant names: Kempinski, Kronprinz, Negresco. "Oh God, how happy I am with you," she had said. "Only you bring me this happiness." He thought he had never properly appreciated these words of hers, but reassured himself with the thought that this was what always seemed to happen in this world.

A fresh gust of wind sent the leaves scurrying round the steel lamp posts. Not just something, but nothing is the same as before, he said to himself.

He had said these words to her as they approached the hotel, and her eyes had quivered, as if she had been found out. "Well . . ." she said. Then suddenly she collected herself. "That's not true for me," she hastily replied. "Not at all."

She repeated what she had said, but her words, instead of reassuring him, pierced his flesh like nails. "Not in my case. Maybe in yours."

"Not for either of us," he replied.

He thought she was awake and he turned his head abruptly, suddenly remembering how his dream about Stalin had continued.

There were just the two of them again, this time at the Novodevichy Convent. It was barely possible to walk through the tightly packed cemetery. Stalin held some flowers in his hand, and seemed to have spent a long time searching for his wife's grave.

He thought, just wait till he orders me, "You lay the flowers. My hand is stiff." But Stalin was angry. His eyes were icy. At least don't let me be there when he overturns the headstone and screams, "Traitor, why did you do this to me?"

He could almost read Stalin's mind. So you complained about my crimes? If you had been truthful, you wouldn't have left me alone. To create havoc. Alone on these steppes. In this horror.

Chapter Two

The same morning. Rovena.

This was the first time that I had pretended to be asleep. Why? I do not know. It just happened that way, like in childhood, when I thought that keeping my eyes shut might give me an advantage over people who were awake.

I felt him touch my hair, and then move the sheet to see my belly. It was just at this moment, instead of saying to him "Awake, darling?" that I did the opposite: I squeezed my eyelids tighter. And like in childhood, when I secretly eavesdropped on my parents to find out if they were still angry over my bad behaviour of the day before, I studied not so much him as his back. Everything about him conveyed anger, but I had the impression that his irritation had settled especially on his back.

In fact I had first got to know him through his back. I might say that it wasn't his eyes, his voice or the way he walked that first made an impression on me, as usually happens, but his back.

Anyone hearing this would call me crazy, or a poseur, the sort of person who always wants to seem original. But I am not like that at all.

"You see that person heading for the main gate? That's Besfort Y. – the one they were talking about yesterday. The one who had that quarrel over Israel? That's him, and they'll probably throw him out of the university over it, if not worse."

I was curious to see him, but he passed through the gate without turning his head, so that only the dark oblong of his back remained in my mind. It seemed to me to be carrying a burden, almost theatrically. I sometimes think that my peculiar attraction towards men with problems started on that day.

Now, so many years later, in front of the hotel window, his back was just as blank and uncomprehending. His hurtful words about nothing being the same as before, which even in the restaurant cut her to the quick, were now, coming from his back, ten times worse.

Rovena slowly stirred in bed. But from her new position she could learn nothing more. His back was the same as before, but darker, because of the light from the window. It was as if their entire story had returned to the beginning.

When Rovena had been upset before, she had tried to think of his endearments and their times of pleasure. But now, strangely, she could only think of their quarrels, which had mainly happened on the phone. These, when Rovena told Shpresa about them, became encrusted with things she had never managed to say but only thought. He rejected her continual complaints about his masterful nature. ("You have made me a slave. You found me when I was young. You treat me as you please.")

"He says that vain men secretly like to hear this – but he finds it depressing. Making a slave of someone is nothing to boast about. It's what all the mustachioed men of the Balkans and the East do. It's so hard to quarrel with him. Sometimes in the middle of a fight you want to embrace him."

At such moments, try as she might, Rovena could not cope with the tide of her emotion. She kept thinking: he has me in chains. He calls me a princess, but in fact he knows very well that he is the prince and I am only a slave. "I keep telling myself this, but it changes nothing. Do you understand?" Her friend from Berne replied that it was hard to know what she meant.

"I understand you when you say that together you get on wonderfully and then you quarrel on the phone, although, in my case, with the man I have, the opposite happens – we say sweet nothings on the phone and as soon as we see each other we're at each other's throats. I understand that bit, darling, but the other things, about slaves and masters, seem way over the top."

"I know, I know, that's how other people's problems always seem." Sometimes, explaining a quarrel to her girlfriend was more exhausting than the original argument itself. "I'm trying to tell you simply that he's preventing me from living my life. I'm not saying he does this on purpose, but the truth is that he has me tied hand and foot and he won't let me go. His life is going downhill. Mine isn't, and he only drags me after him.

He doesn't think of me, how young I am, the sacrifices I'm making.

"As I said before, the problem is that it's hard to quarrel with him, and still harder to win. Once I sobbed out that I had given him my entire youth and asked nothing in return and he replied coldly that he had also given me the best part of his life." That was how their arguments usually ended. After them he would move on, confident that she would follow. Because he had known from the start that she would follow him, while she had only realised this later, and, crazy as she was, had not only admitted as much to him, but had also written it in letters. Did she understand now?

"No. I don't understand you," was her friend's reply. "You told me the opposite in your letters. You wrote that you were happy, madly in love. After all, every one of us expects this from life, to fall in love. There's something unpleasant about this expression, looked at from the outside. Falling in love. A bit like falling into a pit, a trap, a kind of servitude. You have every right to get angry with this man Besfort if he treats you badly. But you have no right to get angry about the things that made you fall in love with him in the first place. You should thank him. And if you decide suddenly that this relationship is a mistake, then that's your fault and not his. Rovena, darling, I don't understand these things you say. Maybe there are other things that you're not telling me. I don't think you know yourself what you want."

This was in fact the truth: Rovena did not know what she wanted. His jealousy made her angry, but his indifference infuriated her even more. During one of her outbursts about this infamous obstacle that prevented her from living, after his bitter retort, "Aha, so you've got some adventure in mind," he had uttered the hateful phrase: "Do what you want. We've never promised fidelity."

Really? she said to herself. Is that all I mean to you? Just you wait and see.

For days the sour aftertaste of this phone conversation lingered. You will see, she repeated to herself. The day will come and you'll throw off your mask.

In the midst of her anger, she wondered what that day would be like and what lay behind this mask – and she longed to find out.

He still stood motionless by the window, or rather his back did.

Rovena made a final effort to sleep, even for a few minutes, in the hope of giving the day a different beginning. Like every day of crisis, it was starting badly. A few happy memories were not enough to put it back on course, as she used to imagine. Her memory of the first morning, for instance, when she had woken up in love with Besfort. No doubt the best part of every love story. Towards dawn, alone, in front of your new master. In other words, the tyrant you have fashioned for yourself. The curtains of the room, and your hair on the pillow, the longing in your breasts, all these things that he took one by one into his custody, were transformed.

She could not summon that day to mind, or rather did not want to. A messed-up day like this one called for different memories, of triumph and the spicy taste of revenge, of Lulu's soft lips as they first kissed in the car, of the music to which she freely allowed the Slovak student to caress her on the dance floor. The first time in her life that she had kissed a woman, and the first time she had been with another man since she met Besfort.

Some vague fear kept her from concentrating. The direction her memories had taken was not a good omen. They say that memories become more intense before a break-up.

She knew this, but there was nothing she could do. She could not endure this fear, with its threat of emptiness. It was worse than the fear when Lulu had first warned her against him. "Listen, darling, and don't think I am just jealous. I really am jealous, and I'm not hiding it, but jealousy would never make me warn somebody that they might be murdered. I know you don't believe me, but from all you say he has all the marks of a murderer. That is what murderers are like these days, all sorts of surprising people. You can be murdered by the last person you expect, your financial adviser or piano tuner, or the priest who says mass on Sunday. Don't be misled by his white shirts, his ties and those briefcases with the EU logo. Darling, I'm not paranoid, believe me. I know from experience what they are like. That special whiteness of your skin scares me. It tempts *that sort* of person."

Lulu only hinted at what she meant by this, for all Rovena's questioning. According to her, there was a kind of lustrous pallor which was particularly attractive to unstable minds.

The door creaked and she opened her eyes. He was no longer

by the window. He must have gone down to drink a coffee, something he often did lately.

Now that he was gone, her mind seemed able to range more freely.

She imagined him sitting pensively at the corner of the bar, as he had done long ago at the café in the Palace of Culture. She had recognised him from a distance on one of his visits to the university over that problem that seemed to drag on without end, but this was the first time that she had looked at him calmly, as he sat with his coffee cup.

This time it had been Rovena who explained to her girlfriend, with whom she was sitting and eating ice cream, the mystery of this man who had got into trouble over Israel, or rather over a chess tournament that he was not supposed to play, or not supposed to lose, she wasn't sure. It was a complicated business. Perhaps he wasn't supposed to win it.

"You've got me confused. Is he a chess player? You said he was going to teach international law. What a blank look he has. It must be because of what has happened."

"No, I don't think he's a professional player, but I think there are foreigners in the tournaments. You think he has a blank look? It's that vacancy that I particularly like."

"I think he's got under your skin," said her friend.

Rovena replied, "I don't know. Perhaps he has. But it was so impossible."

"What was impossible?"

"Everything. Starting from his coming to the faculty, where we had all expected him . . ."

"Of course it was impossible, after that . . . mistake," said her friend.

The rattling of the chains dragging the dictator's statue through the centre of Tirana kept interrupting her thoughts. It was this sound, louder than any earthquake, that divided past from present. Everything that had once been impossible suddenly became real, such as his invitation over dinner, a week after they had met, to a three-day conference in a Central European city.

She had said nothing. She had lowered her eyes in shame and a mist had crept over the evening after dinner, and over the whole world.

All through that sleepless night, the same questions turned feverishly round in my brain. What was this invitation? Was it sexual? Of course it was. What else could it be? Alone in a hotel. Three days, in other words three nights, with a man that you have still not embraced. Oh God, it couldn't mean anything else. And she started again: what if he didn't mean what she thought? What if they didn't share a room? But of course they would. It could only be a double room. A double bed too.

One week later, he told me on the telephone in a restrained, almost cold, voice that the tickets had arrived. He left me no time to reply, or even feel a rush of anger. In an almost seigneurial fashion, he was issuing to a young woman an invitation for a trip, for love, for sex. Curtly, he informed me where he would give me my ticket and told me the departure date.

All my protests starting with "How dare he . . .?" were useless and insincere. Obediently, with head bowed, for all my pretensions to be a young woman of discrimination, I went to the Café Europa, where he was waiting with the ticket. It hadn't been as difficult as I expected to justify the trip. Remember that flood of invitations from associations, NGOs, religious sects, minority groups, all those "alternative" types. "Be careful they're not a group of lesbians," said my fiancé with a supposedly knowing grin. One week later, my face drained by insomnia, I found myself at Rinas Airport. We greeted each other from a distance. He had a brooding look, and I liked that. I could have borne anything at that moment except small talk.

It was a day of fog and rain. The aircraft barely carved its way through the clouds. I was totally numb. The journey seemed endless . . . At one point I wanted to leave my seat and sit next to him, so that I could at least lay my head on his shoulder before we crashed.

After our arrival in the evening, still strangers, we at last found ourselves in the taxi heading towards the great city. The headlights of oncoming cars slid past, in turn lighting up his face and leaving it in darkness, as if it were a mask.

We did not speak. He put his arm round my shoulder. I limply waited for him to kiss me, but this did not happen. He seemed even more dazed and absent than I was.

For a moment, my gaze caught the eyes of the driver in the rear-view mirror. He seemed to be staring at me instead of the road. I knew that this was because I was tired, but I moved aside slightly to be out of his line of vision. Besfort felt my movement and drew me closer. But still we did not embrace. In the hotel room, as we opened our bags, we seemed not to look at each other.

In the late-night bar, we kissed for the first time. I was about to say something, but instead blurted out something else entirely: "My fiancé and I haven't taken precautions recently . . ."

There was no taking back what I'd said. It seemed to me later that it was these words that melted everything away.

His eyes were fixed on my knees, as if he was seeing them for the first time. I felt his stare penetrate the black fabric of my miniskirt to the point where my thighs met, where he was now invited to enter without protection . . .

"Shall we go upstairs?" he said after a short time.

Freed from shame, and with reddened cheeks, I did not hide my eagerness. Let's go upstairs as fast as we can, to the seventh floor, seventh heaven . . .

When I came out of the bathroom and lay down beside him, before removing the towel from my chest, I whispered, "Am I too thin?"

He did not understand what I said, or pretended not to. We caressed each other and I thought of the words of Zara the gypsy woman, yet I could not say them for shame, however much I might have wanted to. But he looked at me for a moment in surprise, as if I had spoken them. A special light, of desire mixed with exultation, seemed to flash through his eyes, or perhaps I only took it as such, out of surprise or because of his words, "My little darling." After our caresses, he was at first a little inhibited, but then everything went well.

It was only later, after I had returned to Albania, that fear gripped me. He had accompanied me to the airport before continuing his own journey to Brussels, where he was to stay two weeks for his work.

There was no word from him for a long time. I was obsessed with all the usual speculations of a woman who gives herself to a man for the first time and wants at all costs to be appreciated. Had it been wonderful for him, as they say, or did I disappoint him, even slightly? Were those sweet words of his sincere? Was his initial inhibition the usual kind of tension experienced by modern men, no longer the shame it once was, but even rather chic, or was it a sign of disenchantment?

The thought that the journey had been a mistake stabbed at me incessantly. I would have given anything not to have made that trip.

I felt a pain in my chest, slight at first, but later more noticeable, sometimes on the side of the heart and sometimes on the opposite side, and I liked to think of this as a sign from him. I was not naïve enough to think that love could really cause pain in my breasts. But I preferred to believe that I was in love rather than pregnant, although this was also a thought that occurred to me, but without distress, as if it were happening to a different body.

*　　*　　*

The window frame was still empty, without his silhouette. She thought of getting up, taking a shower, putting on her make-up and, made beautiful for the new day, waiting for him on

65

the settee. She rehearsed the procedures in her mind, but, still hungry for sleep, turned her body over to the other side. Instead of sleep there came to her a kind of by-product, a drowsy vision of the lane alongside her school, where, just past the slogan, "The People Do What the Party Says; The Party Does What the People Want", clumsily written on a wall, stood the low house of Zara the gypsy woman, with a persimmon tree in the yard. During the long holiday afternoons, like many other girls, she had entered the gypsy woman's dilapidated door without anybody much noticing. The whole atmosphere was different there: the smell of ashes in the hearth, the photos on the wall and especially the conversation, which was like nothing else. With faces crimson from shame, the girls asked all kinds of questions about love, or what the gypsy woman called "fun". She would answer calmly, never showing annoyance, in terms that made your entire body tremble. "Breasts and buttocks? Of course we know what makes them swell – fun. And if you think you are skinny, listen to Zara. Men who appreciate these things go crazy for thighs like yours." Rovena thought her knees would give way. "Don't be stingy with it," she heard the woman say, pointing below her stomach. "Be generous. We'll all be in the grave one day."

These words turned all the films she had ever seen and all the books they had studied at school on their head. A few weeks later, with a new confidence in her movements, she bent down to embrace her and whispered in her ear, "I've done it . . ." The woman closed her eyes in happiness.

Then she motioned to her to come close again. She seemed to want Rovena to tell her what had happened but in different words. And Rovena did so. Bluntly, in words considered dirty, and which she had never used before, she said, "I've . . ."

"You're a real star," said the gypsy woman softly, and her tired eyes and wrinkled face glowed.

That was two months before the December day when the gypsy woman was interned. A purge was under way against vice. Women suspected of loose morals, homosexuals, gamblers and people who encouraged degeneracy were also carted off. Zara belonged to the last category. Criminal investigators in beige suits cropped up on school premises. In panic, Rovena accepted a proposal from a student she barely knew. She thought that this was the best form of safety. I'm not a virgin, she whispered in his ear on the first afternoon when they had gone to bed. He pretended not to hear her.

When the regime fell, she was engaged. Every day, long-forgotten things reappeared out of the mists. Words like "lady", "miss", "your grace", forms of baptism and prayer. But the word "engagement" was one of those that slipped out of use. "Engaged?" asked her girlfriends at the university, with undisguised amazement. To her, the word seemed like a worn-out garment. She used it less and less, and then not at all.

And now you say that nothing is like it was before, she said to herself. That was true then. Everything changed completely, but now . . . Oh God, what about now? Was everything now the same?

In fact, her meeting with Besfort at that reception turned her life upside-down even more than the fall of the regime. He was frank in his admiration for her, and invited her to one of those dinners that were so common in the frenetic Tirana of the time.

When they met face to face again, their conversation turned once more to beautiful women. He made it no secret that he was talking about her, and nor did she pretend not to notice it. She had known for a long time that she was beautiful.

Enthralled, I heard him say that beautiful women, as distinct from pretty ones, were very rare. According to him, they were different in every respect. They thought differently, loved differently and even suffered in a way that was absolutely different.

I could not take my eyes away from him, until, after a prolonged stare in my direction, which was not his usual style, he said to me, "You know how to suffer."

Psychic, I thought. How did he know?

I must have frozen, because he hastened to add, "Does that offend you?"

In fact it had seemed to me a kind of insult, I replied. I was beautiful, and there did not appear to be any reason why I should know suffering. Suffering was for others.

Reading my mind, and doubly psychic, he said that nobody should be ashamed of suffering. Then in a voice that struck me as cold he added that what he had said was intended as flattery, because he was sure there were no beautiful women who did not know how to suffer.

I blushed for what I had said, which now seemed to me idiotic. Attempting to make amends, I added a further idiocy: I did not think that I was that sort of person.

He smiled to himself and shook his head several times, like someone faced with a misunderstanding too radical to be explained.

After a silence, as if suddenly remembering that I was still very young and entirely without experience compared to himself, he added, "I'm sorry, I didn't mean to offend you." Then, without the slightest sarcasm, he said that the ability to endure suffering was a gift, especially the high-class suffering of beautiful women.

Grateful for this respite, I smiled at him and said, "Are you encouraging me to suffer?" And, looking him knowingly in the eye, I added, "Perhaps you don't have to . . ."

I need no encouragement. I will suffer for you. That's what I wanted to say, but I lapsed into silence.

He kept his eyes lowered, and I sensed that he had taken these words for what they were: an open declaration of love.

Before we parted, in a relaxed and almost boisterous tone, he said that if I were willing he could take me on a three-day trip to a Central European city. Half in fun and half in earnest, we played for a while with this idea, which would have been lunacy even a short a time ago in Albania, but now, after the fall of communism, was perfectly realistic. As we parted, he looked me in the eye for a long time before saying, "I'm serious. Just don't say no in a hurry."

I said nothing. I lowered my eyes in shame, and the night and the whole world misted over.

Two weeks later, what had seemed the most impossible thing in the world became reality.

On that day heavy with mist and rain, the Tirana–Vienna flight seemed barely able to move forward. Rovena felt totally numb ... The journey seemed endless ... At one point she wanted to leave her seat and sit next to him, so that they would at least be together before they crashed ...

That is how she told the story later. But in fact she had been alone on that aircraft – not with Besfort at all. The truth was that during the flight she had longed to be with him so much that her mind had gradually performed the necessary changes, to make credible to herself, and later to others, the altered account of the journey.

Its essence remained unchanged. She was going to meet Besfort Y. in Vienna, and during the flight, as the aircraft lurched, she often imagined herself with her head resting on his shoulder. Next to her sat not Besfort Y. but a woman, an activist in the same NGO where Rovena worked. The truth was that she had not hurried to the Café Europa to collect the ticket from him, and he had not suggested they travel together. On the contrary, she herself, after learning of his business in Brussels, had said that she too was going on a trip, to Vienna. "Really? Vienna?" He often passed through Vienna. They might meet. And so, casually, as if playing a game, they had exchanged phone numbers.

In Vienna, after they arrived at the hotel, her travelling

companion's eyes had widened when she announced quite calmly, "I have a lover here. He's coming to fetch me in an hour."

And in front of the woman's very eyes, quite unconcernedly, she started to apply her make-up.

Chapter Three

The same morning. Rovena again.

She shivered, as if a stranger had entered the room. Then she calmed down. It was no one, and Besfort was still not back. The pressure on her temples told her how tired that pretence of sleep had made her.

He is mad, she thought.

Moving towards the bathroom, she did not know why she had thought this. It was something they said to each other so often that it had come to sound like affection.

Under the jet of the shower, the phrase "nothing is the same as before" glittered like a false diamond. It seemed to hang there, as if rinsed by the water.

She was losing the grip on her thoughts of a few minutes before. They were vague at the edges, and even pretending to be asleep had given everything a certain haziness.

The handle of the shower seemed stuck. She thought of what had happened after she came back from Vienna. She was sure that her body had changed, as if her pallor had been absorbed deep beneath her skin and her small breasts, smoothed by desire, no longer belonged to this world. She had felt sure that they had grown since she had first met him. Her feeling of a miracle having happened was mixed with the anxiety that he would not phone and they would part without him seeing them. She imagined him phoning on one of those March afternoons, and then her hurrying to meet him, quickly undressing. Then his admiration, his asking if she had been taking hormones, and her answer that it was nothing like that. "It is you and you alone."

Under his incredulous gaze her words would cover every fault line of fear like mist. It is you and you alone. My fear of you. My crazy, inhuman desire to please you. A mute entreaty. A prayer, as if before an altar.

Perhaps he would remain unmoved, not be as thrilled as he should be, and for all his fine words about marble and the divine, he might still seem to be elsewhere.

She did not want to come down to earth, and so found excuses for him. You have set me free. Other thoughts swarmed or froze in her mind. Would anybody else notice the change? Of course, and very soon. Starting with her fiancé. She had not slept with him since she came back from abroad. She made every kind of excuse. Finally, she met him.

"Do you think I have changed?" she asked.

He looked at her in wonder, touching her fearfully.

She added carelessly, "You don't think I've had plastic surgery!"

"Why not? It's the fashion now. I don't know what else to

make of your trip abroad. It was the first thing I thought of when I saw your breasts."

"How can you be so simple? Don't you see there's no scar! Couldn't you think of any other reason? For instance that I might have fallen in love?"

He stared at her in shock, as if hearing something very unusual.

It seemed that nobody believed in love any longer. There were three or four men who still drifted through her memory like shadows. The gypsy woman's advice long ago had been, "Men are different from one another, and what one man's tool won't do, another man's will!", and so she had gone with these men once or twice. Now, as she brought them to mind, she wondered if she would want to show this change to any of them. The first, who had taken her virginity, had gone off on a boat to Italy. The next was apparently in prison, and the third had ended up a deputy minister. The last had been a foreign diplomat.

Besfort was still in Strasbourg. The afternoons were harder to endure than the evenings. Staring fixedly at the windowpanes, she would ask why. Why did she want to do this at any cost? Was she still spurred on by what Zara had said, "Be generous. We'll all be in the grave one day," or was there some other reason? Sometimes she seemed to be saying farewell to the world before shutting herself away in a convent.

The pitiless afternoons dragged on. On one of them, she went for a coffee in the Rogner Hotel with the foreign diplomat. His conversation, which she used to listen to with such interest, was boring. He mentioned the only time they had met in his apartment. "How wonderful that was," he said. He said it again, but these words saddened rather than excited her. They brought no thrill. In the end, with a serious look, he admitted that he was "bi". Fortunately Albania was changing and it was nothing awful now to be "bi". At this point she thought she dimly understood something. When they parted, he said that he hoped they would meet again. He looked serious again and said something about "new experiences" and "wonderful". She nodded in agreement, but thought to herself, no way.

Walking home, she remembered that the gypsy woman's house must be nearby. There were all kinds of new buildings in the neighbourhood, but she recognised the dilapidated door from the persimmon in the yard.

With an anxious heart, she pushed open the gate. Had the gypsy returned from her internment? Did she bear a grudge? As she was about to push open the house door, she noticed the familiar smell of long ago, a kind of sourness of straw mixed with smoke.

The gypsy woman was there. The same close eyes among the wrinkles looked her up and down.

"Zara, it's Rovena. Do you remember me?"

The wrinkles moved slowly. "Rovena . . . of course I remember you. I remember all of you little angels, my only joy."

Rovena had expected her to say: "You little whores, who betrayed me." But the woman had said nothing of the sort.

Rovena could not find the right words. Did you suffer a lot, where they sent you? Did you blame us? Perhaps nobody had betrayed her. Maybe the harm had been done in all innocence.

Zara's eyes softened a little.

"You are the first one to visit . . ." That was all she said, but her words suggested she had been waiting. "I knew you would. I put my hopes in you. More than in the others."

Rovena wanted to fall to her knees, to beg forgiveness.

The wrinkles slowly melted away, leaving the eyes clear, like long ago. Oh God, thought Rovena, she's turning back into the woman she was . . .

"Where I went, they were all . . ." she said in a low voice. "But what about you, here? What have you been up to, girl . . . Have you had fun?"

Rovena nodded. "Yes, Zara, a lot . . . And now I have fallen in love."

The woman stared at her for so long that Rovena thought she had not heard her.

"I've fallen in *love*," she repeated.

"It's the same thing," the woman said, in the same soft voice.

Rovena felt that they were getting close to her secret. During one of their sleepless nights, Besfort had talked about the millions of years when love had only been lust.

Apparently this was why the way she talked was so mysteriously attractive. The gypsy was carrying her back to her own distant era.

Covered in confusion, and under the woman's now haggard gaze, Rovena took off her pullover, stiffly, as if carrying out a ritual. Then she lowered her underwear, showing the woman her pubic hair. Poker-straight, as if waiting for a jury to pronounce her guilt or innocence, she stood there a long time.

Walking home as dusk fell, it seemed to her that she had undressed for reasons that were as inevitable as they were inexplicable. She had done it naturally, as if obeying a mystical instruction: show your allegiance!

Obscurely, she struggled to understand something that still eluded her grasp. It apparently had to do with the female's different outlook, which had descended from the world of the gypsies, that epoch millions of years ago, as Besfort had put it, and which the *gadji* had forgotten. Indomitable, a superior power attached to a woman's body by a secret pact, it stubbornly guarded its independence. Thousands of decrees had been issued against it. Cathedrals, internment camps, entire bodies of doctrine. In the last few days, Rovena had felt that this power could rise from its lair and overwhelm her.

Reaching home, her feet carried her to the sofa. She wearily calculated the days until Besfort's return.

Meeting him was different from how she had imagined it. He seemed distracted, gloomy, as if he had brought with him the cloud cover of the continent.

A vague fear stalked her. This man who she liked to think had brought her freedom might unthinkingly take it from her again.

You're dangerous, she thought, as she whispered into his ear tender words about missing him, about her visit to the gypsy woman's house and of course her coffee with the man she now called the "bi-diplomat". Some good had come out of that cup of coffee. She had heard about an Austrian scholarship to go to Graz, and the "bi" had said she could apply.

"It would be easier for us to meet in hotels in Europe, wouldn't

it, where you might have things to do, and I could come . . .
aren't you pleased?"

"Of course I'm pleased. Who said I wasn't?"

"You don't look pleased."

"Perhaps because while you were talking I was thinking . . .
sort of . . . about how girls today think nothing of going to bed
with someone for a visa or a scholarship . . ."

She broke off, lost for words. He touched her cheeks, as if
tears lay on them.

"How beautiful your eyes are when you have things on your
mind."

"Really?" she said, not thinking.

"I was asking you seriously," he went on. "Shall we do it?"

Oh God, she thought. "I don't think so," she blurted out.

He did not take his eyes off her, and she added, "I don't
know . . ."

Tenderly, he kissed her hair.

"You were going to say something, Besfort, weren't you?"

He nodded. "But I don't know if we should always say
everything we think of."

"Why not?" said Rovena. "Perhaps it's not a good idea
generally, but we are, kind of . . . in love . . ."

He laughed out loud. "A moment ago, when you were so
honest, I thought of how honesty makes a woman look beautiful.
But sometimes, unfortunately, an unfaithful woman can look
just as beautiful."

"What do you mean?"

"Don't scowl. I wanted to say that treachery generally makes someone look ugly. That expression, the evil eye, has some truth behind it. But an unfaithful woman can look wonderfully attractive. We're in love, aren't we? You said yourself that everything is different . . . in love."

His voice was carefree, unlike an hour before, but still dangerous, she said to herself. He behaves like someone not afraid of going to the edge. Why is it he feels safe and I don't? The thought made her irritable. She wanted to ask, in annoyance: "What makes you feel so secure? Why do you think I belong to you?"

She knew that she didn't dare ask. She lived in fear and he did not, that was the difference between them, and as long as this did not change she would feel defeated.

She murmured softly as he stroked her chest, and he asked her to tell him again what the gypsy had said.

"I can see you like to make fun of her."

"Not at all," he retorted. "If anybody treats the gypsies and the Roma with respect at last, it is us at the Council of Europe."

As if frightened of silence, she went on talking as she combed her hair at the mirror. He stood by the door, studying her now familiar movements.

Putting on her lipstick, she turned her head to say something, her tone suddenly altered, about her fiancé. Her internship in Austria would inevitably take her away from him and they would separate.

She looked at him closely to see what he was thinking. He was careful to say nothing, but took two steps towards her and kissed her on the neck. "We'll be happy together," she whispered.

Later, she regretted saying this. He should have been the one to say it. As always, she rushed in too fast.

What did she need all this for, she groaned to herself. She thought she had left qualms of this sort behind, but they were still there, especially during the last moments of every meeting: things that shouldn't have happened so abruptly, things there was no time to put right. He put it down to anxiety before they parted. She could not work out whether it was better to say as little as possible to avoid misunderstanding, or the opposite, to gabble nervously to fill up the frightening void. She now knew that just before they said goodbye there would come a fatal moment that would decide what shape her suffering would take until they met again.

All these misgivings belonged to the past, but they still insistently fired their darts from a distance. She wanted to say to them: "All right, I've remembered you now. Leave me in peace."

She arrived in Graz in midwinter, soaked by the rain that poured from the February clouds. The fog banks watched her like hyenas. The house where Lasgush Poradeci had lived was gone. She had thought that Graz would make an impression on her, at least as strong as that left by Besfort Y. But the opposite happened. Her breasts grew smoother.

His phone call rescued her from the barren winter. He was not far away. He would expect her at the hotel on Saturday. She should take a taxi from the station and not worry about the expense.

They spent two nights together, and she repeated endlessly,

"How happy I am with you." Then she travelled back to winter and the tedium of her hall of residence.

She stood motionless for a moment, holding the shower head above her hair. The water splashed either scalding or icy and gave her no pleasure. It was the first time a shower had failed to calm her. Then she understood why: the shower head reminded her of the telephone.

That was where the friction usually started. The first and most serious incident had been in spring. Everything had changed in Graz. For the first time, she hankered after liberty. She grew irritated for no reason. She thought that Besfort stood in her way.

These were her first cross words on the phone. "You're preventing me from living."

"What?" he replied coolly. "I'm getting in your way?"

"Precisely. You said that you tried to phone me twice yesterday evening."

"So what?" he said.

She heard the unconcern in his voice, but instead of kicking herself for her blunder, she cried, "You're holding me hostage."

"Aha," he said.

"What's that 'aha'? You think that I have to sit waiting in until it occurs to his lordship to phone?"

"You don't know what you're saying," he butted in.

Her ears rang with shock. "You think I'm your slave. You think you can do what you want with me."

"You don't know what you're saying," he repeated, his voice growing colder.

Sensing the approaching danger, she lost control completely. The words poured out of her until he cried, "That's enough!"

She didn't know he could be so pitiless. He was totally cynical: "You took this yoke up yourself, and now you blame me." To cap it all, the line went dead.

Numbly, she waited for him to phone back. Then she gave up hope and called his number herself. His phone was off the hook. Now what have I done, she thought. And then, a moment later: this is horrible.

She racked her brains all night, trying to work out why she was so angry with him. Because she had left her fiancé for him, although he was promising her nothing?

Perhaps, she thought. But she was not sure. Nor was it fear of losing her freedom. Was it because she had fallen into this head first, and now could not get out? It was too early to say.

She reassured herself, saying this could all be sorted out calmly if she tried to love him less. That was the solution.

Three days later, she admitted defeat and phoned him. He answered her stumbling phrases sternly but quietly. Neither of them mentioned the quarrel. Several weeks passed like this, with infrequent phone calls and guarded conversations, until they met again.

The train to Luxembourg crossed the cold European plains. The landscape, dusted with snow, matched her inner numbness perfectly. Was everything the same as before or not? He had given nothing away on the phone. She and her fiancé had behaved quite differently. After making up, they used to have heart-to-hearts, confessing how hurt they had felt and describing their ploys in battle, which reconciliation had made redundant.

Darling, why do you make it so difficult? she thought, as she dozed in her seat.

The further north the train sped, the more terror overcame her. But something within her also resisted this fear, a peculiar, unfamiliar taste, provoked by the thought that she was a young and beautiful woman travelling through a frost-covered Europe towards her lover.

She was still half-dazed when the train arrived.

He waited for her in the hotel room. They embraced as if nothing had happened. For a short while, she rushed round unpacking her things, making only a few comments about the room, then about the bathroom and the white dressing gowns that always struck her as the sign of a good hotel.

When she ran out of words, she made no effort to find new ones. It was nearly four o'clock. The winter dusk was falling. She said, as usual, "Shall I get ready?" and went into the bathroom.

She could not tell how long she should stay there. Usually she seemed either too quick or too slow.

Finally, she wrapped the bath robe round her naked body and came out.

He was waiting.

With head bowed, she moved towards the bed. Her steps did not seem her own. She could not get rid of the strange sensation she had felt during the journey, which was mixed with the feeling that she was less like a girlfriend than a wife going to bed with her husband.

For some reason she tried to contain her cries, and almost succeeded. But afterwards she whispered in his ear, "That was heavenly." That was how it always seemed to him. But they did not open up to one another. When this didn't happen at midnight, nor before they parted the next day, she gave up all hope. As her train travelled across those same plains which the torn mask of snow could not totally cover, her heart felt heavy with the same sadness as two days before. It was so hard to deal with that she did not know if sadness was the right name for it.

Her misery was accompanied by a nagging thought that Besfort Y. was dangerous under any circumstances. Life with him was difficult, but without him it was impossible.

With her former fiancé, restoring normality after a quarrel had been a matter of moments, but with Besfort it took months. She sometimes wondered whether this question of freedom had turned into an obsession. Since the fall of communism everything in Albania had gone to extremes: money, luxury, lesbian groups. Everybody was in a hurry to make up for lost time. One afternoon in a café, an actress's sidelong glance had stirred her to the depths. From the way Besfort responded to this story, she thought she must have put her finger on something.

Then, too, nothing had been the same as before, she thought. But she hadn't said anything. She hadn't shouted it to high heaven as he had.

In fact, nothing had ever been the same as before, she thought. She recalled her first infidelity – only in Albanian did it deserve the name – as a hurried mess, vindictive and without regrets. Kisses amidst music and accented German. Shamelessly groping her partner before he lunged at her. Undressing in the bedroom, the condom, then his accented words: *Ich hatte noch nie schöneren Sex*. That was the best sex I've ever had.

That's all you're getting, she said to herself.

In fact, it was a year after Luxembourg that she told him what had happened in that spring of temptation. The little birthday party in her hall of residence, embracing a classmate on the dance floor, pressing first her lips and then her belly to his, then his whispered invitation, "Let's go to my room." She had followed him without a word. Besfort knew everything that happened between then and the next day, when half the student group gathered in a late-night bar and Rovena was astonished to find that a miniature love story had already been woven around her. They had found out that the pretty Albanian girl had *finally* slept with their Slovak friend. They gave them special attention, made sure they sat next to each other and treated them as a couple in every respect. She found it amusing and not in the least embarrassing that this engagement business followed her everywhere she went. Somebody said that on the news there had been disturbances in Albania, but she knew nothing about this.

What happened later, you know as well as I do, Rovena had said. In fact, what Besfort knew was not quite the truth. The inaccuracies started in the late-night bar, where Rovena and the Slovak were being treated as a couple. She liked him, in fact she liked him a lot. He tasted different, and had a kind of sweetness that she missed. Somebody said again that there was unrest in Albania. But she still knew nothing.

At two in the morning they noisily departed, arranging to meet the next day in the same bar. At ten in the morning the telephone tore into her sleep and ripped everything apart. It was Besfort. He had phoned her several times during the evening. She could not be irritated again, or use the stale words "You're preventing me from living." He was in Vienna, at an OSCE meeting. Things looked bad in Albania, as she may have heard. He was free that evening. For the first time she hesitated.

"Why didn't you tell me before?" The journey was hard for her . . . the seminar . . . the professor . . .

"As you like."

The chill in his voice brought back her old fear. "Wait a moment, could you come here?"

"I don't know," he replied. He would see what he could do and phone back.

He did not call back for a long time. There was no reply from his mobile. He must be punishing her for hesitating. Tyrant, she thought. Then she turned against herself. See what she'd done. She had risked everything for a night out. As if there hadn't been enough boring evenings in Graz, she had chosen this one to trawl through the bars with their cheap jokes and laughter, just at a time when he needed her.

Finally the phone rang – a double triumph. He was coming. The address of the hotel? What time?

She strode briskly down the frozen street as if intoxicated. The pang of conscience over the date she had made at the bar increased her exhilaration. Even her hesitation towards Besfort seemed to her a good sign. For the first time in eighteen months she felt, if not the superior, at least the equal of Besfort Y. The issue about being his slave would resolve itself naturally.

Her sense of security, flattered by the luxurious carpet in the long corridor leading to his room, was dashed by the expression on his face.

His frown did not emphasise his tiredness but had the opposite effect, perhaps because of the vacancy in his eyes, that aspect of him that was so impersonal.

They lay on the sofa clasped in a half-embrace. He still suspects nothing. Why not? she thought. Why does he still think he owns me?

That vacancy in his eyes still troubled her.

In the bathroom, as she was getting ready, she noticed a dark bruise at the top of her thigh, a mark left by the Slovak's teeth.

Secretly, she wanted him to notice this. Does this persuade you that you don't own me? This is crazy, she thought. Behind the closed door, she heard the phone ring.

When she came out of the bathroom he was still talking.

"What's going on?" she asked as she lay down beside him.

He stroked her, not answering. They made love, almost without speaking. In the restaurant, as she glanced at the expensive menu, she remembered that by now the others would be meeting in the late-night bar. They would look at her empty seat for ages before realising she wasn't coming. And even then they would never understand the truth. They would think that she had followed the standard pattern, rejecting the poor student with the soul of an artist, with whom she would share the cost of a pizza, in favour of luxury and a man with power.

They can think what they like. The red wine and the crimson nail varnish of her fingers holding the glass provoked the gentle intoxication that was so delicious before making love. After dinner they sat for a while in the bar.

"Don't even think about it," she said to him, caressing his hand. And when he asked about what, she continued, "You know what. The bad news, down there."

The phone rang again after midnight. How dreadful, she groaned, not surfacing enough from sleep to realise what time it was. Two in the morning. Was he crazy? He was talking. Whoever it was calling him at that hour must be out of their mind. In vain, she buried her head in the pillow. She could hear everything. "I think it's a communist uprising . . . Yes, I'm sure . . . reclaiming power by force . . . Of course it's terrible . . ."

Despite her annoyance, she was curious to listen. She understood only half of what he said. "Intervention is the only solution. Immediately. Couldn't it be seen as an invasion? . . . By whom? . . . Aha . . . at one time it would have been, but not now . . ."

When he put down the phone, she sat up, leaning on her elbow. "Brussels?" she asked.

"Yes," he said. He added, "There's been a coup in Albania."

"That's what I thought." For a while the only sound was their breathing. "Would you support military intervention?"

He nodded, "I don't think I'm wrong."

"In the old days that would have been called treason," she said. "They talked about nothing else at school."

"I know."

She stroked his hair. "Don't worry, darling. It's past two o'clock."

In the bar they were now surely wishing one another goodnight. They would guess at all kinds of reasons for her absence, but never imagine that she was in bed with a man who had been talking on the phone about things that would hit the front pages of the papers tomorrow.

Tomorrow she too might find it hard to believe. It was easy to say that she had exchanged poverty with its pizzas for a life of luxury. But it was something else. He had made her more complicated. He had turned her into a beautiful, mysterious woman, the kind she had dreamed about as a schoolgirl.

An unfamiliar kind of lassitude clung to her body. She embraced him gently, murmuring loving words into his ear. Don't think about what's going on down there. She had a feeling everything would be all right. Nobody would call it an invasion. She was ready to die for him. Come, darling.

Afterwards, in that lightning-scorched clarity of mind that only follows sexual release, she was stabbed by an unaccustomed pang of regret that he was not her husband. As she fell asleep, the cavernous sense of irreversible loss abated, and it seemed natural to think that, quite apart from what the law stated, he was in truth her husband.

After breakfast she told him that she would go to her seminar, to put in an appearance, and come back as soon as possible.

It was more annoying than she expected to be pestered by questions about where she had spent the previous evening.

"We looked for you everywhere, we expected you. You might have let me know," said the Slovak.

"I couldn't," she said. "Somebody arrived unexpectedly from Albania. There's been a coup there."

"Oh, so that's what's on your mind," he continued.

"Of course."

He shrugged his shoulders. Since he had left, he hadn't given a thought to Slovakia. He never wanted to hear the place mentioned again.

She knew this. A lot of Albanians talked like this.

An hour later, as she almost ran to the hotel, the March wind did all it could to draw out her tears. The two receptionists gave her a strange look. One of them handed her a small envelope.

"My darling, I've had to leave suddenly. You can imagine why. xxx B."

The tears finally poured from her.

With a sudden movement, as if finding the lever to stem the flow of her memories, Rovena turned off the shower.

The silence was worse. She was sure that he had still not come back to the room. To fill the emptiness she picked up the hairdryer. A wild blast of air replaced the rush of the shower, a suitable accompaniment to her fury.

You're finally going to tell me what it is that isn't the same as before, she thought angrily.

They had been together so many years and yet she had

never said those words to him. Not during the nightmare of The Hague, on the threshold of the great trial. Not even during the worst storms at the time of her relationship with Lulu.

Throughout that winter, the cold eyes of the psychiatrist had looked at her, sometimes to the right and sometimes to the left of the mirror. "This sort of crisis is not common, but it is well documented. You are making a passage, undergoing a transition. Because this experience is over, you think you have accomplished it painlessly. You forget that even moving house is a form of stress, let alone what you're going through now. It's like being transported to another planet."

After leaving the doctor, she vented half her anger on the phone, right there in the street. "I've changed now, understand? You're no longer what you were to me. You aren't my master any more, understand? Nor as frightening as I used to think, not any more."

Nothing was the same as before . . . She had once said to Besfort these same words that now, from him, wounded her so deeply. Perhaps it was now his turn.

Take your revenge then. What are you waiting for? The deafening noise did not allow her to calm down. But the thought occurred to her that he was not the sort of person to take revenge by giving as good as he got.

As long as he has not made the same switch, she thought. The Council of Europe was said to be swarming with gays.

The silence after she switched off the hairdryer was twice as deep as after the shower.

Just . . . as long as he . . . has not . . . meanwhile . . . made the same switch.

Her final words fell slowly like the last leaves after a storm has abated.

In the silence she felt defenceless again. Her eyes darted to her cosmetics, spread out below the mirror. First she reached for her lipstick. She lifted it to her mouth, but in her nervous haste allowed the tube to slip to one side. The red smudge goaded her into daubing herself even more crudely, instead of taking proper care.

I can be a murderer too, she said to herself . . . Like you, my lord and master.

The noise of the door brought her up short. He's back, she cried to herself, and half her rage evaporated instantly.

Hurriedly, as if destroying the evidence, she wiped the lipstick from her face.

She grew calmer as she started on her eyelashes. The ritual of make-up always cleared her mind more than anything else.

She thought she could muster a smile, but her face still did not obey.

She felt safe with the idea that the more beautiful she made herself, the more easily she could extract his secret. A mask always gives you an advantage over an opponent.

Chapter Four

The same day. Both together.

Just as she had expected, he looked admiringly when he saw her.

"Now I know why you're so late."

"Have you been waiting a long time?"

He looked at his watch. "About twenty minutes."

"Really?"

He had drunk a coffee downstairs and returned while she was in the shower.

"It's beautiful out on the balcony. But what's the matter?"

She raised her hands to her cheeks. "I don't know, but I felt ... I remembered for some reason that old gypsy woman. Do you remember her? I told you about her. She was interned because of us."

"Of course I remember her. Perhaps it was my fault. I promised to do something for her. There were compensation schemes and special pensions for these cases. Give me her name and address. I won't forget this time."

"If she's still alive," she said. "She was called Zara Zyberi."
She knew the name of her street, Him Kolli, but not the number.
She remembered only a persimmon tree in the yard.

She watched his hand writing this down and could barely
hold back her tears.

After breakfast they went out for a walk, following their daily
routine. Finding a suitable café was so much easier in Vienna
than anywhere else.

Outside the cathedral, the old-fashioned carriages waited for
passing tourists. Seven years before, they too had taken one. It
had been midwinter. Under the dusting of snow the statues had
seemed to make tentative signs of welcome. She thought she
had never seen so many hotels and streets with "prince" or
"crown" in their names. It was her last hope that he would think
of marriage, but instead he started talking about the overthrow
of the Habsburgs, the only dynasty to fall without bloodshed.

In the café, they watched each other's hand movements and
fell silent. The small ruby of her ring sparkled like frost.

For some reason he recalled the posters of the last city elec-
tions in Tirana, and the Piazza restaurant where an Italian–
Albanian priest had suddenly struck up the song "There by the
village stream, the last Jorgo fell".

He wanted to tell her about the extraordinary insults the
candidates had thrown at one another, and especially about
that unknown villager Jorgo, who was mentioned in the song
as if he belonged to some dynasty, as Jorgo III or XIV. But at
that moment any connection between the memories of the
posters and the drunk priest evaporated, the warm glow had

vanished from her face and a veil of sadness had descended. Also, he had not had time to tell her the dream about Stalin.

She did not hide her sudden change of mood. After nine years together, and all she had given to this man, he had no grounds to upbraid her over such things. Nor did he have any right to torment her with ambiguous remarks.

He knew that this was a most inadvisable time to say, "What's the matter with you?" But the words burst out of him.

She smiled wanly. "You should ask yourself that." He had said that nothing was the same as before, and she had a right to know what this meant. She had waited a whole night to find out.

He bit his lower lip. Rovena stared at him.

"You're right," he said. "But believe me, it's not easy for me to say."

The chill descended again at once.

Then don't say it, she wanted to cry, but her lips did not obey her.

"Is there someone else?" she blurted out.

Oh God, came the lacerating thought through his mind. This old phrase, rising from the grave. It wasn't Rovena who had used it long ago, but himself.

He remembered the scene. As vividly as the election posters, the dilapidated telephone box outside the post office, the filthy rain and her silence down the phone.

"What's the matter with you?" he had asked, and Rovena had said nothing. And then he had almost shrieked, "Is there someone else?"

They were still using the same words, as if they had no right to any others. "Is there someone else? I'm giving you an answer. There isn't."

The tension suddenly eased, and she closed her eyes. She wanted to rest her head on his shoulder. His words came to her as if through a soothing mist. There was no other woman. It was something else. She translated this into German as if to grasp its meaning better. *Es ist anders.*

Let it be anything, she thought, but not that.

"It's more complicated," he went on.

"You don't love me in the way you used to? You're tired of me?"

It's not about me. It's to do with both of us. It's about the freedom that she often complained about . . . He had decided to tell her, but now he found he couldn't. Something was missing. A lot of things. Next time he would manage it. If not, he would try to put it in a letter.

"Perhaps it's not true? Perhaps it only seems that way to you? Just as it seemed to me?"

"What did it seem to you?"

"Well, that things aren't the same as before. I mean that there is something that isn't like it was, and so it seems to you that everything has changed."

"That's not it," he replied.

His voice seemed to echo as if from a church belfry.

She thought that she had grasped his meaning, but it evaporated in an instant. Was it that he felt tied, in the same way as she had, and wanted to break free? She had once shouted at him: "Tyrant, slave-owner!" All this time, had he too been chafing in silence at the enslaving chains?

As always, she felt that she was too late.

He felt tired. His head ached. On the street, the illuminated signs above the hotels and shops glittered menacingly.

He recollected not the lunch with Stalin, but her first letter. Icy, sub-zero Tirana finally seemed to be getting serious. That's what she wrote. And as for the place below her belly, since he asked for news of it, it was horribly dark down there.

He remembered other parts of her letter, in which she wrote about her waiting, about her coffee with the gypsy woman, who had said some things that she could not put on paper, and again about the sub-zero temperatures in which all these things were taking place.

Smiling wanly like the winter sun, they both recollected almost the entire letter. In his reply from Brussels he had written that this was without doubt the most beautiful letter to have reached the north that year, from the remotest part of the conti-nent – the Western Balkans, which was so keen to join Europe.

Later, when they met, he was eager to hear what the gypsy woman had said. There was another form of desire, he said, which came from a mysterious, remote epoch.

She wanted to weep. Remembering old love letters was not a good sign.

He had wanted her to tell him about the gypsy woman when they were in bed, before they made love. She told him in a low voice, as if whispering a prayer. He wanted to know if the gypsy woman had asked to see between her legs, and she replied that she hadn't needed to because she had opened them herself, she could not tell why, she just did it, like the other time . . . oh no, she didn't seem lesbian. Or rather, in the fug of that house, lesbianism might be mixed with other things . . . you really are psychic . . .

After lunch, they both wanted to rest. When they went out again, dusk had fallen. The royal crowns above the hotel entrances, which in other countries had all been effaced, still wearily clung on in their niches.

They found themselves outside St. Stephen's Cathedral again, at the end of the boulevard. In the dusk, its windows cast assorted reflections, as if trying on different masks. They looked like the dead, sometimes coming back to life, and sometimes vanishing again.

Bending over her shoulder, he whispered loving words which now sounded incredible to her ears, so rare had they become. First he had stopped saying them. Then she had given up too.

Like forgotten music, they returned, but they seemed somehow unreal. We have lost our feeling for each other, he said in an even sweeter voice. Astonishingly, these words did not sound frightening to her, although they should have done. Nor did the word "marriage" when he uttered it. It seemed untrue, like in a dream. They had been in Vienna seven years before, and she had waited for that word in vain. Now it had arrived after so long, but in an unexpected form.

"Will you agree to be my ex-wife?"

She wanted to cut him short. Was he crazy? But she thought it was better to wait. This was not the first time that he had been obscure. During one of their arguments on the phone, she had said to him: "You tell me to look for a therapist, but you need one more than I do."

"Your ex-wife?" she finally interrupted. "Is that what you said, or did I mishear you?"

Gently he kissed her and told her not to take it the wrong way. It had to do with their conversation a while ago.

Aha, so we're back on that subject.

His voice sank to a low murmur, like before their first kiss. She should try to understand him. Their time of love, if not over, was approaching its end. Most misunderstandings and dramas happened because people did not want to accept this end. They could easily tell day from night or summer from winter, but they were blind to the end of love. And so they could not face up to it.

"Do you want us to separate? Why not just say so?"

He said that she was using the world's usual standards. Just like the rabble do. All the world's ordinary opinions, which unfortunately are the most widespread and claim the authority of laws, come from the rabble. He wanted to get away from that sort of thing, to find some chink through which they could escape.

Rovena made no further effort to understand him. Perhaps it helps him to talk like this, she thought. He said that the two of them were going through a period of transition. Later, the last glimmer of their love, like the final rays of the sun, would fade. Then a different, negative time would begin. This time was ruled by different laws, of a kind that people rebelled against. They fought against them, suffered, hit out at each other, until one day they realised to their horror that their love had turned to ashes.

Go on, she thought. Don't lose your thread.

Of course, it was already late for them. But he particularly wanted to avoid this kind of end. He did not want to enter that twilit world. He wanted to find another path, while there was still light. Perhaps we should interpret the descent of Orpheus into hell to bring back Eurydice in a different way. It was not Eurydice that died, but their love. And Orpheus, trying to bring her back, made a mistake. He was in too much of a hurry, and he lost her again.

It was you who told me that love is problematic in itself, she thought. A long time ago he had said: "There are two things in the world that are in doubt: love and God. There is a third thing, death, which we can only know through seeing it happen to other people."

Two years before, at the height of her affair with Lulu, he had forgiven all her harsh words, because she had seemed to him insane. Now she would do the same for him. He seemed exhausted, and of course his nerves were in a bad way.

In the hotel, after dinner, he had eyed the receptionist suspiciously as he asked, "Is there any message for me?"

"Who are you expecting a message from?" she asked.

He smiled. "I'm expecting a summons. A court summons."

"Really?" she said, trying to maintain the same tone of mockery.

"I'm not joking. I really do expect a summons. To the Last Judgement, perhaps . . ."

He avoided her eyes in the elevator mirror.

"They'll find me in the end," he said softly.

"You're tired, Besfort," she said, leaning her head on his shoulder. "You need to rest, darling."

In bed she tried to be as loving as she could. She whispered words of endearment, some of them laden with the double meanings that he enjoyed so much before lovemaking, and then, after he sank exhausted beside her, she asked in a very quiet voice: "What was it you said . . . your ex-wife?"

His reply came in the same breath as his final sigh.

"Sublime," Rovena repeated to herself.

Increasingly his thoughts reverted to the strange taste of their first meeting after the episode with Liza. He knew that something had happened, but could not tell what, especially not that a woman had come between them.

Under the pale illumination of the lampshade, her face sometimes looked as strange and inscrutable as it had then. The hope of experiencing that feeling again was like waiting to recapture a dream of incommunicable sweetness, of the kind that other, gentler worlds seem to grant only once to a human life, and then purely by chance.

Evidently Liza had been part of the transition that was vital to the creation of this strange zone.

"What did you think?" asked Rovena, about when he interrogated her on the subject of Liza.

He tried to laugh it off, and said, "Nothing," but she was no longer smiling.

"You're still hiding something from me," she said in a weary voice. "Don't you think you're going too far?"

"Possibly. But I don't feel guilty about it."

He said he didn't feel guilty because, however secretive a man was, or pretended to be, he would always be an amateur compared to a woman.

"Women are the soul of secrecy and, like it or not, so are you," he whispered, caressing her below her belly. "Nobody, not even a woman herself, can ever know what is hidden behind that silent entrance. Unless the gypsy woman's eye can see it."

As she listened, she suddenly remembered the girls' lavatory at school, where someone had scrawled, "Rovena, I'm dying for your c—." Shocked, she had gone back to the classroom, totally unable to guess which of the girls might have written it. Perhaps this one, and then perhaps another. After each suspicion came the same question: how could this other girl know about her private parts? Nobody had ever touched them, or even seen them, apart from her mother. She had hurried to the lavatory again in the next break, but the writing was gone. On the roughly whitewashed door a piece of paper was pinned, "Wet Paint."

"Don't think I'm trying to be mysterious," he said, stroking her hair. She kissed his hand. Oh no. He didn't need to try, he just was.

Hidden under the coat of paint, the scribble seemed much more threatening, and as she returned to the classroom she felt her knees give way.

He promised that this mystery would pass and that next time they met everything would be clear.

"You always put off everything until next time," she complained. "Do you really expect a summons? Is nothing really the same as before? At least tell me that."

He did not reply at once. He touched her hair, and strands fell over her eyes like a veil. In a clear voice he said that this was the truth.

Chapter Five

Thirty-three weeks before. Liza, according to Besfort.

All the reports claimed that Besfort was in Tirana thirty-three weeks before the accident. The few opulent skyscrapers belligerently reflected the summer light off one another. As he walked through the once forbidden neighbourhood, unable to decide upon a café, it seemed to Besfort Y. that the very glass of the buildings expressed the city's malice and its troubled conscience, as vented every morning by the newspapers. Lawsuits, grudges, debts, unsettled feuds that bided their time – they were all there.

He stopped hesitantly outside the Café Manhattan, weighed up its neighbour and, without further thought, entered the Sky Tower.

The view from the enclosed terrace on the sixteenth floor was beautiful at any time of year. From this height, the journalists' speculations seemed more credible: the owners of the first four storeys of the Sky Tower, including the café where Besfort was sitting, were fighting a court case with the state. At the foot of the tower were the foundations of another skyscraper, whose builders were in conflict with the landowners, the city council and the Swiss Embassy, on whose land they were accused of encroaching. A little further on was a statue, also a subject of dispute, involving historical symbols and, indeed, indirectly, the clash of civilisations and the attack on the twin towers in New York.

Besfort Y. could not suppress a sigh. Then he heard a mixture of Albanian and German from the next table.

"Albania wears you down," a friend of his had said, after leaving for Belgium in 1990. "She drives you to despair and sends you round the bend, but there's no escaping her."

They both thought the same. The more you insult the place, the more it tightens its grip on you. It's like the love of a whore, said his friend.

Rovena was back in Graz. She had managed to extend her stay for the third time. "For your sake," she said on the phone.

He looked out of the corner of his eye at the next table. One of the foreigners might be the "bi". Besfort stared at his chin and the reddish curls at his temples, considering if this man had really slept with Rovena. My darling, he said to himself. How had she put up with all of that?

A wave of longing gently enveloped him. He must get down to writing that letter he had promised her when they last met.

There was movement at the next table, and heads turned towards the window. Besfort looked in the same direction. The columns of traffic in both directions had been halted on the main boulevard. Someone pointed out a crowd that formed a dark mass on Mother Teresa Square.

"Another demonstration," said the waiter, removing the ashtray. "They want their property back."

The placards bobbed white but illegible above the crowd. In front of the prime minister's office, a second row of helmeted policemen quickly lined up.

Besfort ordered a second coffee.

He had better write that letter soon, he thought. A letter and two or three phone calls would discharge most of the tension. Liza's name, mentioned so often in Vienna, was a suitable peg on which to hang the broken thread of their dialogue.

"No, it's not former property owners," said the waiter, setting down the coffee cup. "They're Çamëria Albanians, angry at the government."

"Which government?" asked Besfort. "The Albanian or the Greek one?"

The waiter shrugged his shoulders.

"Perhaps both. Whenever the two reach an agreement, these people take to the streets."

The demonstration was still too far away to read the placards.

Liza was more than a pretext, he thought. She was perhaps the key to understanding what was happening. It was no coincidence that they had both remembered her again in Vienna, after forgetting about her for so long.

Two years before, after their big quarrel, he had experienced for the first time the taste that comes from making love to a woman you have discovered a second time. It was a mixture of the recollection of the start of the love affair, which was at that moment ending, with the beginning of something else. It was her taste, and yet not hers at all. She was his, but not his. She was a stranger, yet familiar in every nuance. Actual and ineffable. Faithful and elusive.

Ever since their last meeting, his mind had harked back continually to everything to do with that feeling. His dream of resurrection certainly had something to do with it. As a student at the university, he had studied Albanian folklore, with its motifs of rediscovery. Now for the first time he wondered at their mysteriousness. The bridegroom in his marriage bed who recognises by a birthmark that his bride is his sister. Or conversely, the bride who recognises her brother. The father who returns from exile and takes his son for his enemy, or his enemy for his son, and so forth, all these stories of incest which were thought to be fiction, but very probably were not. All these violations of taboos, obscure desires within the tribe, which out of shame or horror were passed on as legends, floated to the surface of his memory.

"You're no longer my master. I won't stand your tyranny any longer. I've had enough."

Besfort turned his head to the window, as if Rovena's voice on the telephone two years ago, racked by sobs, now came to him from outside.

The crowd of demonstrators was now close to the prime minister's office, and their shouts were clearly audible.

"It's not about property, or Çamëria," said the waiter, also looking out of the window.

The placards were mainly pink.

"I think they're the 'alternatives'," said someone at the next table. "That's what the gays and lesbians are called now."

Rovena's voice on the phone was no longer recognisable. Taken aback, he was stuck for words. He interrupted her, "Calm down, listen to me." But she snapped back, "No, I won't calm down, I won't listen to you."

He hung up in fury, but she called back at once.

"Don't hang up like you always do. You're no longer . . ."

"That's enough," he shouted back. "You're not in your right mind."

"Really?" she said. "Is that how you think of me? Now listen. Get ready to hear something very serious."

You aren't what you were to me any more. I love someone else. Amidst the deafening crackles and abrupt silences of the telephone line, those were the words he expected. But amazingly, something else came down the wire.

"You've ruined my sex life."

"What?"

The thought that her mental health was not good suddenly took priority over everything else. Everything she had said, her insults, even her possible infidelities meant nothing. He tried to handle her gently. "Rovena, my dear, calm down. It must be my fault, no doubt about it, my fault, only mine, are you listening?"

"No, I'm not listening. And I don't want to. And don't think that you're as frightening as you seem."

"Of course I'm not, and I don't want to seem frightening."

"Really?"

"You think I'm trying to scare you? You think I'm like an American Indian, tattooing my face to look fierce?"

Amazingly, she laughed. He even thought he caught the word "darling" smothered by her laughter, as so often when she liked one of his jokes. But she was quiet only for a moment. Her voice rose stridently again, and he thought, oh God, she's really not well.

The next day she seemed more relaxed on the phone, if a bit tired. She had been to the doctor, who had asked some tactful questions. She explained that she had quarrelled with her lover. The doctor had given her tranquillisers and some advice: most importantly to break off all contact with the source of the trouble, in other words with him. A long silence followed.

"Are you going to ask the same old question, is there anybody between us?"

"No, I'm not," he answered.

"You say not, but you're thinking it. Because you still don't understand that I'm no longer your slave."

He let her say her piece. She said he had enslaved her. He had closed every door that opened for her, and not allowed her the slightest freedom. He wanted her entirely for himself, like every tyrant. He had made her seek therapy. He had crippled her, he had ruined her sex life.

He butted in to say that the opposite was true, that he, or rather both of them, as she had said time and again, had refined their sex life to a degree that few others had achieved. But that, she protested, is precisely what should not have happened. He had violated her nature . . . her psyche.

"Is that the twaddle your German doctor talks?" he interrupted.

"Precisely that," came her answer.

He imagined her breasts, and the insult and pain he felt at the prospect of never seeing them again made his response unexpectedly quiet. He would leave her in peace, but she should understand one thing, that her description of him was unfair. He had been her liberator, but this was not the first time in history that a liberator had been taken for a tyrant, just as many a tyrant had been taken for a liberator.

That was more or less all he said. Her next telephone call three weeks later came to him as if from a great distance. Her voice was different. Neither of them mentioned the quarrel. She said that she'd been in London with the rest of her course group. That she had taken up sport, mainly swimming. It was as if nothing had happened. Only when she asked, "Are we going to see each other?" a silence fell.

"What do you think?" he asked.

Her reply was unexpected: "I don't know."

He almost shouted, "Then what the hell are you calling for? Why ask if we are going to see each other?"

"Listen," she went on. "I want us to meet, like before, but I don't want to lie to you . . . Something has happened . . ."

So that was it. In the long silence that followed, she seemed to be waiting for the question whose time had finally come. Is there somebody else? But he said nothing. He had asked this question at the wrong time, and now that its hour had struck he kept his silence. Slut, he said to himself. NGO whore. International scholarship tart. But aloud he said, "I don't want to know."

Her own reply was also slow in coming. Perhaps she expected something else, or took his answer as a sign he didn't care. "Really? So you don't want to know? OK, I'll give you the whole bitter truth: you are no longer what you were. I belong to someone else."

"I realise that. I've known for some time . . ."

She wanted to reply: "But you pretend not to care. That's how you usually behave. You hit back at someone else when you're on the ropes yourself." But she did not utter this final retort out loud. Her unspoken words flew round her brain like lost birds that could not find their way out. He listened to her laboured breathing, until finally she said, "If that's the case, then come here . . ."

The flight was tiring. The plane listed perpetually to one side, or so it seemed to him. It was literally a lame journey. Drowsily he imagined her in front of the mirror, getting ready for another man. Choosing lingerie. Her armpits, between her legs. An unnatural faintness, at the same time a burning and a weakness, slowed his heartbeat. If it was another man who had caused this estrangement, why should she be so angry with him? The anger should be on his side.

The flight was like a journey in a dream, in which arrival is indefinitely deferred.

He saw her from a distance, waiting in the same place as always. Her paleness made her even more beautiful. She had changed her hairstyle, and lowered her head in a different way as she walked.

They embraced hesitantly in the taxi, as if through glass. She was the same and not the same. Words beginning with "re"– recognition, resurrection – sprung to mind. They would haunt him for days. He had thought that he would never arrive, but now the prospect of going to bed with her seemed even more remote.

She had booked the hotel. He would try to get his bearings from its layout – the entrance, the lobby and of course the room with its big double bed, or two single beds, like the two graves of former lovers he had once seen in a Japanese ceme- tery in Kyoto, with a marble headstone on which was carved the couple's sad tale.

As the bellboy opened the door to the room, his heartbeat slowed again. The room was flooded with tranquil light, and he saw the large bed with its counterpane decorated with drooping chrysanthemums, again like on Japanese vases. She seemed to belong to this kind of world as she padded softly back and forth, unpacking her bag in silence, as if she were painted on a vase. "Will you wait a bit for me?" she said with bowed head as she entered the bathroom, without her playful look that usually augured happiness.

Here was the mystery that had lured him for so long, he thought, as she closed the bathroom door. It seemed impossl- ible that she would ever come out again in the way she used to.

He sat on the corner of the bed, as if in that Kyoto graveyard, waiting for his bride, or like in 1913, or God knew when – a man of the Balkans with the pent-up lust of years of betrothal. Or worse, like a madman who believes his lost bride, abducted by someone else, or by destiny itself, will return to him.

Finally she emerged. Oh heaven, a total stranger, as pale as plaster, just like a real bride under traditional law. With head bowed, she approached the bed and lay down stiffly beside him. It seemed to him that they had forgotten entirely how to move. He bent down over her face. Her lips, like her eyes, looked alien, and he did not kiss them but whispered, "Has anybody else touched these?"

She said yes with a motion of her eyes.

The open bathrobe revealed her breasts, which were perhaps even more complicit in the conspiracy than her lips. He asked his question again, and her reply was the same.

He was not sure his body could withstand the swoon, in which misery was mixed inextricably with desire. And who was the lucky man, he thought.

He caressed her belly, and then below. When he asked his question again, she made the same motion of her eyes. So you've gone all the way, he thought, but what he said was, "Which means . . .?

Rovena did not answer. She stifled a groan, in a way she had never done before, as if sucking it inside, and he said to himself: of course.

Instead of music, a distant police siren accompanied their last moments of lovemaking.

* * *

116

A siren from nearby suddenly interrupted Besfort's thoughts. It was almost the same sound as on that night in Luxembourg. He smiled, remembering that the Albanian police had been supplied with new cars from the West: their sirens had brought the first hint of Europe to Tirana. He turned to the window to look. Skirmishes had broken out on the main boulevard. They're throwing tear gas, said someone who had been close by. People could be seen lifting their hands to their eyes, as if scared of shadows. The bi-diplomat's curly hair looked as if it had caught fire. He remembered that redheads were sexually insatiable. My poor darling, he said to himself, who knows what you put up with from him.

That was more or less what had passed through his mind when, after their lovemaking, he collapsed exhausted alongside her.

Her words on the phone, mixed with others that were the product of his imagination, came back confusedly to his mind, with altered syntax, like a ritual formula. My sex life has been ruined by you.

Other men have abused you and you blame me, he thought. After their lovemaking, he had repeated his unanswered question. Had she gone the whole way? She hesitated again, before saying, "It depends what you mean."

In a soft voice, so as not to disturb their stillness, he had said that this made no sense. The other man, if he had kissed and caressed her everywhere, had certainly gone the whole way . . . as they say.

She gave the same answer. "It depends what you mean."

"How?" he asked. "Was he impotent?"

"No," Rovena replied after a long silence. "It was a woman."

He poured his entire being into a long release of breath. So this was the truth. He experienced a few moments of total perplexity, and then he thought he had found the answer that explained everything. Questions rushed pell-mell to his mind. If it had been a woman that had tempted her, why had this infatuation, this new-found desire engendered such fury against himself? And why all this suffering and shouting, that visit to the psychiatrist?

She listened in astonishment. "What do you mean, why? It was only natural that this should happen. I wanted to break away from you and you wouldn't let me. I wasn't double-crossing you, do you understand? That's all."

It all became clear to him. As if her confession had been some opiate, his head fell back onto the pillow. She too wanted to sleep. They were both exhausted, and two hours later they woke up as if in a different era. It was as if he was discovering her again. But still he was not sure. It was like an image on the surface of water, which the slightest ripple could destroy.

Cautiously he took up the conversation where they had left off. He heard Liza's name for the first time, and about the circumstances of their meeting. The nightclub where she played the piano on Saturdays. Their interlocked stares. The phone call. Their first kiss in the car.

Then? Then we know the rest.

"I don't know anything," he had said with childish curiosity. "Tell me everything . . . Tell me how you did it."

"How we did it? . . . In fact I didn't do anything. She was the one who . . . I just let her . . ."

Rovena went on talking. Her description was earthier than anything he had ever heard. Did she get these words from the gypsy woman?

"Tell me again," he had said, almost pleading. "Tell me everything."

She told him about how as a schoolgirl she would get excited in gym class when the girls undressed. Apparently she had the instinct at that time, but not in any special way, only like many girls. She wasn't lesbian, as he might think. It was more an escape from her fear of men, caused by anxiety over her breasts, which she thought were smaller than they should be. With Liza, she had become even more of a woman.

More of a woman, he thought. How much further could she go?

For the first time, she kissed him on the neck, but coldly. "After all, everything I have done, everything so far has been for you."

He went back to what he had said just after their lovemaking. Still panting fast, he had said that she blamed him for everything that had happened to her. If she was attracted by a woman, discovered a new experience or melted in a rapture of desire, it was his fault. In the middle of this upheaval she had gone to a psychiatrist, for reasons that remained obscure, and this too was supposed to be on his conscience. She expected him to repent and ask forgiveness.

He had expressed to her only a part of all this, vaguely and incompletely. She had listened in silence, and then with the same gentleness had said: "That is the truth. It was for you."

Besfort could not get angry. But his voice was still cold.

"Tell me something. But clearly and accurately. When you told the psychiatrist why you were upset, and that you had quarrelled with your lover, what form did you use, masculine or feminine? I think they are different in German."

She sighed. She didn't deny that there had been friction with Liza. But it was always over him. He had captured her like a songbird and would not let her go. She was trying to escape from his cage, but couldn't. So she quarrelled with her girl-friend . . . Flailed. Injured her wings. Screamed.

All their conversations about Liza were disjointed like this. It wasn't just Rovena. He too was in no hurry, almost as if he was scared of the fog clearing. It took a long time for him to reclaim Rovena, and he was not sure which he preferred, the first Rovena, so lucid, or this second one, so awkward, with her plaster mask and a double life.

Whenever she came close to him again, within reach and laughing as before, he felt, alongside the delight of rediscovery, a regret as the mask melted away. How could he bring back that otherworldly taste that came from alien, infinite regions?

One evening, as he stared at a sex doll in the window of a sex shop in Luxembourg, she had taunted him: "Go on, buy it, if you fancy it so much."

"I will buy it," he had answered earnestly. "But on one condition, that it's just like you."

Rovena had scowled, not knowing how to take this.

He could not totally explain it either. He did not want to disturb that veil of mystery that had fallen over her since the episode with Liza. Yet he knew that it was impossible not to do so. The weeks passed and they grew as close as before. It was a miracle, he repeated to himself, but deep down he felt that it was not so much a miracle as a kind of calm.

"You're fed up with me," she said, "so you want the company of a mask. Why don't you find one of those Japanese actresses caked with plaster of Paris, a mystery within a mystery, like sleeping with a bride who has risen from her coffin. Isn't that what you're looking for?"

He had come to the conclusion that he could not experience this dream-like sensation except with a person who had once been close to him but was now distant. He would make Rovena a stranger again, like two years before. He would lose her in order to win her again.

He was aware that these were crazy ideas, contradictory notions.

Perhaps he should take tranquillisers to keep this kind of excitement under control. And not drink so much coffee.

The temptation to play a game with Rovena, like Russian roulette, perhaps really came from another dimension. But her obsession with freedom, where did that come from? These things were somehow connected to each other, and so was his question: does love exist?

He thought with a smile that there were cases in which freedom could also be granted by force. He ordered a third coffee, but dared not touch it.

On the boulevard, the street sweepers were clearing away rubbish and placards that had been trampled underfoot in the fray. This short eruption of anger had subsided and its traces were being removed, leaving behind the old, familiar rancour of court cases and disputes over ancient wills, some of them in dead languages and with Ottoman seals.

Chapter Six

The end of the same week. Rovena.

All week she had been worrying and trying to ease her mind by phoning regularly. But these frequent calls only increased her distress. The opposite tactic of not phoning at all only made things worse.

We shouldn't have talked so much about Liza, she thought. Neither of them had given her a thought for almost two years, and suddenly, like a baleful ghost, she had come back to haunt them when they met in Vienna.

Sometimes I think that you purposely never wanted to hear all about her. You wanted to torture me with unasked questions, with suspicions that I might think you still harboured secretly.

I have started so many letters about this and torn them up. I have worn myself out brooding over it in solitude. I tried to explain when we were together, but you were always impatient to reach the climax, the only part that interested you. You tried to look as if you were listening but you were not. Your eyes were always glazed when I described the nightclub where I met Liza, and how she kept her beer glass beside the piano.

My inner confusion, her look, my answering stare, then the kiss in the car, her hand on my thigh, the memory of the school lavatory, and my hand taking hers to lead it between my legs, then her groan and my opening the zip so she could find what she was looking for . . .

Feverishly, you kept asking the same questions, and only those: "When you opened the zip, did you know what she wanted?" Then you would keep talking without listening to my reply. "Tell me, when she had you in her hands, I don't know if you would put it that way, I mean when she had taken you completely, as you might say . . ."

After I finished describing our lovemaking, you lost interest, so I could never explain that I went with Liza not because of that instinct of so long ago, but because I wanted to loosen myself a little from you. Subconsciously I wanted a woman more than a man. I did it for my own sake, perhaps because it was an easier way out. It was easier that way, perhaps because there couldn't be any comparison between you. But, believe me, it was more for your sake than mine. So as not to injure you with a rival. But the devil got into you and you started phoning more often at the very time when I needed a little rest and distance from you. You called every day, which you had never done before. These were the first weeks with Liza, and we had our first quarrel over you. She became jealous of you, and spent hours spinning her theory that you were not merely an obstacle in my life but had distorted my real sexuality. I argued back as hard as I could and told her that you had made me twice, three times the woman I was. She ridiculed what she called my naivety and ignorance of the world. She would caress me and murmur in my ear that I was one of the few women with the natural gift to reach the heights of ecstasy that only the gods can imagine, if only I could get rid of that hindrance in my path, meaning you. You, meanwhile, instead of helping me resist this, did the opposite. The more irritated you were on the phone, the sweeter she murmured in my ear, until the day when something incredible happened, the only thing that I have never told you and I'm not sure I should: she proposed marriage.

It happened after an ordinary quarrel in a café, a jealous tiff, initiated by me when I thought she was angling after someone else. To get my own back I pretended to be attracted to someone else too. Both angry at each other, we ended up at her place, and then in bed, where she used all her skill to excite me as never before. We were born for each other, she whispered as she stroked me. I am the pianist, you are the instrument under my fingers, and that's how we will always be. We'll ascend to the divine. We'll climb to that seventh heaven that so many talk about but only a handful of the chosen ever reach. Expert as she was, she uttered the word "marriage" or rather exhaled it at the instant of climax, to associate it with this moment, just as they say sadomasochists do.

Later that afternoon, in the drained and febrile state that you like to call "rainbowed", I went home. I had indeed almost crossed the rainbow and realised my vague adolescent dream, but this time in a different, tangible, purposeful way: I was marrying a woman.

My emotion was mixed with a similarly vague anger towards you, as well as grief and bitterness, because you had never made that proposal to me.

The bridal veil, the wedding guests, everything appeared to me in surreal fantasy, as if from another world. I told myself that this was nothing less than the truth: I would be married on another planet.

Liza and I were going to go to Greece, where, for the last few years, on an island with an abandoned chapel, women had been marrying in semi-secrecy. This would all change soon. The Council of Europe was drafting new legislation and we would no longer have to conceal our relationship on the street, in cafés and at concerts where we could not keep our eyes off each other, she on the stage and me in the audience.

This is what I thought, but meanwhile my pangs of conscience over you gave me no rest. I consoled myself with the idea that I was sacrificing myself for you. Like a bride who marries in another city to prevent her wedding causing pain to her jilted lover, I was marrying into another world, that of women. Or so I liked to think. It was less a joy in itself than a way of side-stepping you, while at the same time avoiding any insult to that other wedding ring, yours, which did not exist.

How I had longed for your proposal during that unforgettable winter trip to Vienna. All the street lights, neon signs and billboards advertised it, shrieked for it. The church bells clamoured for it. You alone were deaf.

I was still in the street, caught between my morbid intoxication, pain at parting from something, fear of what was to come, anger at you and a peculiar hollowness in whose depths lay that illegal chapel, when all of a sudden you phoned.

From the first moment, that phone call struck me as strange and ill-timed. Your voice too. No doubt I replied frostily, which made you say, "What does this tone of voice mean?" Then everything spiralled downwards. The harshness in your voice was only half of it. There was a note of mockery. You ridiculed everything, my emotional state, the bridal veil, the marriage vows, the surreal chapel. Pitiless, destructive, as you are at your worst, you tore all these things apart like rags. Of course I lost control. In the heat of that rage I said those words that wounded you so much, about ruining my sex life. Of course they came from Liza. She insisted that when the memory of men's brutal penetration faded from my violated body I would be ready for a higher plane of love.

To cap it all, two hours later, while I was sitting in despair after my quarrel with you, Liza phoned. She spoke more lovingly than ever and she expected me to reply in kind. My confusion first astonished and then offended her. So you're having second thoughts? You've changed your mind? I couldn't think clearly. She grew angrier. My vacillation disappointed her. She had thought her proposal had made me happy. She had never in her life made such an offer, and now I was being coquettish. "Wait, let me explain," I said, but she was no longer listening. Then she called me unfaithful. I said she didn't know what she was saying, and then she started reviling you. "Go on, go back to that terrorist," she said. "That warmonger will end up on trial at The Hague. And you'll be there with him."

Amazingly, her fury brought me a kind of calm. Especially her parting shot. She had been a pacifist, and therefore opposed to the bombing of Serbia, and when she found out from me the sort of work you did she became all the more pro-Yugoslav out of spite.

At midnight I was still torn by my dilemma. Should I phone you or her? Or rip the phone out of its socket? Tormented by insomnia and a racing pulse, I could hardly wait for morning, to go to the doctor.

True, those were the words I used: "I've quarrelled with my lover." Psychic as you are, later you wanted to know which gender I had used. There's barely a difference in German between *Geliebter* and *Geliebte*. As usual, your question preyed on my mind. I had been honest, and at the same time I had not. I had said *Geliebter*, in the masculine, but in fact the word covered both genders. Liza, more than my *Geliebte*, was also my *Geliebter*.

You changed totally when you heard the word "doctor" that day on the phone. You softened and kept asking for forgiveness. I felt I had become an object of pity. I sobbed and lashed out at you once more. At that moment I realised I had lost the battle. All my words of abuse – tyrant, egotist, brute and more of the same borrowed from Liza – fell like snow on armour plate. Not only did you not notice them, but you even went on begging for forgiveness.

The desolation that descended on me later was terrifying.

The doctor told me that I should keep away from the source of the trouble. A total break. But strangely, I only associated this break with you. Liza was angry with me, but you terrified me.

You had banished me to a desert region, whose silence tortured me more than the uproar of our quarrels. It was a murky area, a sticky mixture of truth and lies. Your notion of forgiveness was also unclear, and founded on ignorance. My unfaithfulness was both true and untrue. So was my marriage to Liza, and everything else.

Now you tell me that nothing between us is the same as before. At the very moment when I was telling myself that after all these upheavals we were, thank God, at peace again, you uttered those words. You asked that frightening question, "Will you be my ex-wife?" and said other mysterious things.

You didn't talk like this when we met after the catastrophe, when I was still numb, as if I had just woken from a dream to find myself lying beside you in our bed of love. In these miraculous twelve years with you, this was without doubt our most fabulous night. You said it was as if I had come from the moon. You said that perhaps this is what it will be like in the future when couples meet, one of them returning from some journey or mission to another planet.

Not even then did you tell me that nothing was the same as before. But now you not only say it, but mean it.

There is something floating in the wind. I can feel it. Just as I feel that I always act too late. You always strike the first blow.

Strike. Do what you have to do. Just do not leave me alone.

This is not a matter of love. It is beyond love. You have invaded me in a way perhaps forbidden by nature's secret laws. They say that between lovers unnatural exchanges often take place across mucous membranes, in a kind of reverse incest, in which the blood of the family and alien blood perversely change places.

If that is so, you must obey other laws. You may be my ex-husband, and you may declare me to be your ex-wife. But if I have mistakenly become your little sister in the meantime, you cannot abandon me here in this world, a blind swallow with broken wings.

You mustn't do that. You can't.

Chapter Seven

Twenty-one weeks before. Snowstorm.

The snow battered the train window with redoubled fury. The thought of that other train, on which Rovena was travelling, not only failed to snap Besfort Y. out of his inertia but also plunged him deeper into his stupor, as if he were dulled by some sedative.

He had done what was necessary. Shortly after midnight, bending over the pillow, above the tangle of her hair. After the final gasp, and almost scared that he had really choked her to death, he had whispered, "Rovena, are you all right?"

She had not answered. He touched her cheeks and whispered words of endearment, which she perhaps took to be the last she would hear from him, because her cheeks slowly dampened with tears. From her whisper, Besfort could only grasp the word "tomorrow". They would leave by different trains the next day, but unlike at other times they would be free of the anguish of separation. Tomorrow, darling, you will feel for the first time what that other zone is like.

For the whole time, almost fifty hours, that they had spent together in Luxembourg they had talked of nothing else. As she listened her eyes became ever sadder. Her objections grew weaker from exhaustion. The dead are also always together. He said no, a thousand times no. They would be free like at the creation of the world. Free, meaning no longer separable. Free to meet if they wanted. To get tired of each other. To forget each other and find each other again. They would experience the revival of desire as no one had ever done before. Whenever they saw each other, they would be strangers, but familiar, as if they had seen each other in dreams. More or less like the time after the episode with Liza, but with a thousand times more power. She should trust him and not harbour dark thoughts as she had done the night before, when she suspected that he was treating her like a call girl or high-class hooker in order to humiliate her, and so, when the time came, to get rid of her more easily. No, he swore he had always wanted the very opposite, to turn her into an icon.

As he talked, her gaze gradually grew pained, insistent, as if she were trying to ask him, Darling, who infected you with this sickness?

Outside, after a lull, the blizzard raged again. A passenger entered the compartment, lurching drunkenly, and glared at Besfort. Unable to contain himself any longer, he said something.

"I don't understand German," Besfort replied.

"Aha," said the man. "So that's what it is." He muttered to himself for a while, and then raised his voice. "But you don't need to know German to know that Luxembourg is a crap place. It pretends to be a little country to excuse its crapness. All the mileage on the road signs is wrong. The banks open their back doors at night to let in reformed paedophiles."

Besfort stood up and went to the buffet car for a coffee.

Perhaps Rovena's train was now out of the storm. He longed to press her head against him. It was like this, with her head leaning against him, that they had fallen asleep after midnight. At about two o'clock, she had woken in fright. "Besfort, Besfort," she had said in a low voice, rousing him. "I want to know – what about our conversations, what will happen to them?"

"What?" he asked, as if caught red-handed in some crime.

"Our conversations, late at night, after we make love."

"Oh yes, of course, our endless conversations," he said. "Don't be frightened. They'll be the same as before."

"Do you mean that, or are you just saying it to keep me happy?"

"Of course I mean it, darling. Everyone knows about conversations between call girls and clients. Geishas too. They produced half the literature of Japan."

"I'm sorry," she said, "perhaps it's my fault for falling asleep. Weren't you saying something about conspiracies? I was twelve years old when there was the last conspiracy in Tirana. I remember, everybody talked about it. My mother was waiting for my father to come home. She asked him even before he took off his coat if there was any news. It was winter. The prime minister had just killed himself. I was thinking more about my breasts, which refused to grow. But what about you? I think you said it upset you a lot."

He replied that this was the truth. It was a sort of grief unlike any other. Like an abyss. A kind of infinite despair. One conspiracy followed another, and with each the abyss yawned wider.

"But why?" she asked. "Why such despair? There was disappointment when they failed, but they must have offered a shred of hope. At least some people were risking their lives to bring down the dictatorship."

He shook his head. "This was precisely what wasn't true. Nobody was trying to do anything. Nobody was risking their lives. The conspiracies were bogus, and the conspirators were play-acting. Is this anything to smile at?"

"Absolutely not," she replied. "It strikes me as very frightening."

"Exactly. They were perhaps the most frightening conspiracies in the world."

In a steady voice he told the story, which seemed to Rovena halfway between a lullaby and a fairy tale.

"There have been bogus conspiracies since the time of Nero, perhaps even before. Conspiracies invented for the sake of an idea. For reasons of state. To overcome a crisis. As a pretext for an attack. For the purposes of terror. Invented out of fear. To forestall an evil. (See how you hatched your plot and still couldn't overthrow me?) Cooked up by women. Out of spite or in madness. The world has seen all kinds of conspiracies but, believe me, none like those of the Albanians. One might well ask why people dreamed them up. Who stood to gain from them? The truth is that nobody stood to gain anything except a bullet in the back of the neck. Everybody knew that. But they continued with their pretence. Do you think I'm imagining all this? Believe me, I'm not exaggerating – if anything, the opposite. So, if they knew what was in store for them, why did these people pretend to be conspirators? People usually pretend to be loyal, not the opposite. And yet these people impersonated traitors. They could not pretend to be loyal, because that is what they were, the most faithful of all. But the dictator was surfeited with them and their love. He wanted something else. Of course you think that this is lunacy. You were thirteen years old when all this ended. You were almost spared it, but I was not. You might still want to find a thread of logic in this tangle. You might think, for instance, that both sides started this business in play, like a piece of theatre. The courtiers would play the roles of plotters, and the dictator would pretend to punish them, until they would all explode with laughter, yawn and wish each other a good night. Knowing the madness of those times, you might imagine that halfway through the entertainment a shadow of doubt would creep into the tyrant's morbid mind, and the actors who had started off chuckling and grinning would end up in handcuffs. There would be a sort of rough logic in that. But the truth beggars belief. It's hard to explain, even impossible.

"At that time, our whole lives were enveloped in lies, like a dense fog obliterating every horizon. There wasn't a glimmer of light anywhere. One after another, plots loomed out of the mist, first vaguely, like the shape of a foetus in its mother's womb, and then in clear outline. Some people still believed that even if one plot failed to topple the dictator the next might have better luck. But each plotter turned out to be more abjectly faithful than the last. The conspirators' letters from prison became more and more ingratiating. Some requested Albanian dictionaries, because they were stuck for words to express their adoration of the leader. Others complained of not being tortured properly. The protocols sent back from firing squads on the barren sandbank by the river told the same story: their victims shouted, 'Long live our leader!', and as they conveyed their last wishes some felt such a burden of guilt that they asked to be killed not by the usual weapons but by anti-tank guns or flamethrowers. Others asked to be bombarded from the air, so that no trace of them would remain, or to be buried head first, or buried alive, or even left as carrion for birds of prey like in ancient times. Nobody could distinguish truth from fiction in these reports, just as it was impossible to discern what the purpose of the conspirators, or even the leader himself, might be. Sometimes the leader's mind was easier to read. He had enslaved the entire nation, and now the adoration of the conspirators would crown his triumph. Some people guessed that he was sated with the love of his loyal followers, and that he now wanted something new and apparently impossible – the love of traitors, behind which the West was hidden, NATO, the CIA, which he had persuaded himself he hated, but in fact secretly loved. Like Tito, his first idol, but later his bête noire, whose memory gnawed at him day and night. His bête noire had crossed the rainbow, while he had been left behind. One imagined him howling during the night – why had the world accepted Tito but not him? Who was standing in his way? And he would guess who: it was his loyal followers, who clung to his coat-tails and would not let him go. At the very foot of the rainbow, they held him back from making that great leap. (You won't allow me to live.) They pinned him by the arms, they clung to his buttons, his bloodstained boots: you belong to us, not them. Do not leave us. He wanted to shriek at his contemptible pack of lackeys: 'It's you who are in my way. (You have destroyed my sex life.) Wait and see.' And he would lash out at them. The more they ingratiated themselves, the harder his whip fell. Then, even as they screamed, he thought they were making fun of him, or so he came to believe. In the end, they were the victors."

Outside, the snowstorm had subsided. Besfort Y. felt tired. He could no longer tell how much of this farrago he had merely rehearsed in his mind, what he had actually told Rovena, and still less how much of it she had listened to.

Towards five o'clock Rovena had stirred in her sleep. Cautiously, he had touched her. "Did something scare you?"

She said something meaningless and whispered drowsily, "Why are you putting me to this test?"

He kept his eyes closed, as if he could answer more easily from behind a mask of sleep.

Why am I doing this? His eyes followed the scattered snowflakes. He would find out why.

He heard the drunk's familiar voice. You don't need to know English, sir, to realise what a crap country this is.

Oh God, he thought. This is all I need. Fortunately, the man had buttonholed a tall red-headed passenger. "Believe me, sir. Europe will become Islamic. And in Arab countries, when the oil runs out, when they're dirt poor, Christianity will take over like two thousand years ago." No, no, the tall man objected, and tried to turn his back on him. But the drunk would not let him. "Are you going to listen to me? I've got something to say. Then Christianity will try to take over Europe, like two thousand years ago, but it will be too late. Understand? Too late! There will be muezzins calling to prayer from the tops of skyscrapers. Too late. Do you understand me? You don't need to understand English to realise what a disaster that would be."

Besfort went in search of another window seat. The last flakes of snow, as if torn from a bridal veil, darted away from him in panic.

Why was he doing this? He had come back to this question so often during those two days with Rovena. At times all his explanations turned to a blur and were meaningless, even to himself. So he tried to think of others. Of course, they would be free. Not just Rovena, but himself too. Both of them. Free from suspicions and pointless jibes. Free from routine, the pressure of rituals, jealousies, the futile irritation of long silences on the phone. Free, finally, from that gorgon, the grim hag of separation. Rovena was trying to follow his thread. Like this, won't you find it easier to leave me? He pretended to laugh. It was not a question of finding it easy or not. They were abolishing separation itself. A call girl and her client, even if they want to, cannot separate. They are already through the looking glass, beyond the reach of so many vanities of this world.

She tried to argue with him, but wearily and without enthusiasm. Was he just trying to rekindle the flame of their desire? So that whenever they met she would be a stranger, more remote and physically more attractive?

He did not know how to respond. He couldn't deny it. In fact, the possibility, even talking about it, was exciting. She said, "No, no," in a plaintive voice that sounded less like an objection than an agony of temptation. From then on he was teased by the suspicion that she too subconsciously liked the idea.

Rovena had asked her question again, and still he could not reply.

"You scare me to death," she had said. "Aren't you afraid, Besfort? You ask for impossible things . .."

He did not know if he was scared or not. He knew it was too late to turn back.

Why was he doing this? It was easy for him to say he didn't know himself. In fact he did know, but was pretending not to. He had always known. He was trying to hide from the reason. But try to avoid it as he might, it was always there.

They had talked about a lot of things, but had left much unsaid and only partially revealed. Of course there was fear. But not of something impossible. There was his fear of her, and hers of him. The fear in both of them.

He had felt this from the first, when she had lightly walked up to him and sat down on the settee at that unforgettable after-dinner meeting. You are more than I can bear, his entire being had cried.

Rovena was too much for him. He felt beyond the law. What

law, he could not identify, but he knew he was beyond some kind of law.

She had said something and he had replied, but his words had no connection with what he was thinking, that no man can ever cope with more than three or four beautiful women in his life. He had already had his share. It was dangerous to hunger after more.

The enigma of beautiful women had fascinated him for years. What were the characteristics which made beautiful women different from pretty ones? Was there a distinction, if only an unstable one, a dividing line like the meniscus on water, or where the two layers of a mirror adhere, which defined their evanescent nature? Whether loyal or unfaithful, they were all the same, always in the clutches of something, someone, caught by some celestial barb of which they themselves were unaware.

In their presence, something still seemed missing. They threw their arms round your neck, spoke loving words, gave themselves to you, but your thirst remained unslaked. He told himself that nothing was missing. He was asking for more than he should. And yet something still percolated across the dividing line, the caresses, the voluptuous tears.

Even when you thought they were defeated by suffering and that they had become like the rest, it was not true. Some protective avatar came to their aid. You thought that she had really been with you, her moans were still in your ears and her tears damp on your cheeks, but meanwhile she had consigned her true self, her indestructible original, to some distant place. And against this you were powerless. And if this drove you to fury,

140

if her lovely neck, her lips, breasts, hips, and the sex which she gave you, were not enough and you sought to extend your dominion over her invisible self, then the only way to do this was through murder.

When he first saw Rovena perched as casually and lightly as a swallow on the sofa, that is how he had pictured her in some dark region of his imagination, like a small bird targeted by a weapon.

Without doubt, she was "one of those". This expression is usually used of whores. But her case was different. She had all the marks of beautiful women, that elusive dividing line, and everything else, in an astral conjunction. To himself he said, no. He had never been the kind to chase women, still less now, and he was not going to resort to pitiful clichés about his heart still being young although his youth was over. He thought that the opposite was true of some men: not the body, but the heart aged first. He was one of them.

When he thought back to that after-dinner meeting, he could never remember the turning point at which he allowed himself to be lured.

The pounding of the train's wheels seemed right for long memories. These events called for that sort of rhythm.

The plain lay half-covered in snow. Which country was he in? The blanket of snow had created a united Europe before the statesmen could shade it on their maps.

The train thrummed monotonously. His cheap little game with Rovena, of the sort played billions of times in this world, lasted much longer than he expected. The young woman suddenly became difficult. In any other case, this resistance would have increased her value, but this time it had the opposite effect. This was how ordinary girls behaved, not "that sort". Beautiful women did not resort to stratagems of this kind, because they did not need to. Rovena was losing her special characteristics. This was why he could invite her on the trip so casually and shamelessly.

In the hotel, he was relieved rather than disappointed when he saw her young girl's breasts. This deficiency seemed sent by the gods to protect him. Pale, delicate, defenceless, she looked less like a dangerous woman than a little martyr.

But this respite was short-lived. A few weeks later, as her breasts bloomed, she had regained everything: the invisible dividing line, the playfulness in her eyes, her mystery. She waited impatiently for him to show his pleasure, but instead he froze. Finally, he produced the word "heavenly", but he knew that he had wanted to use the word for something else, not her swelling breasts.

There was something back to front about this story.

Moreover, Rovena whispered into his ear that these breasts were because of him. This terrified him. He would have found it a thousand times easier to cope with a pregnancy. But this relationship of a different kind, which seemed to involve the female blood line, what Albanian customary law called "the milk line", awoke in him only horror.

Now he was the defenceless one, like after that dinner long ago. And just as when on the sofa she had looked like a bird targeted by a weapon, he heard now an inner voice warning him against this relationship.

Of several dreams that he had had, there was one he particularly did not like to think about. Rovena was trying to peer sidelong at a scar that descended from her throat to her white breasts, a lesion that sometimes resembled the sign of the cross and sometimes a mark of strangulation.

Lulled by the familiar sound of the trains as he crisscrossed Europe on his wearisome journeys, he thought of leaving her dozens of times. Next time, he said to himself. Next time would be the last. The Balkans, meanwhile, were in flames, and so he put it off.

"Did you think about our separating even then? Before you told me that nothing was the same as before? Tell me, please. While we went from one hotel to another, and I thought you were happy, were you getting ready to say this?"

It was hard to answer, impossible.

Who in this world knows what he is getting ready for? You set off in one direction and you know it's wrong, but you pretend to believe you're on the right path.

He had persuaded himself, and later Rovena, that they had gone to the Loreley to rekindle their passion, but deep down they knew it was for another reason. He had wanted to settle accounts in advance – with jealousy, with the pain of separation, with infidelity. Like a boxer in training to take punches without getting badly hurt, he would grit his teeth and prepare to see her in the arms of another man, before his very eyes.

Once he had outfaced all these lesser fiends, Rovena herself, when the time came, would pose no danger to him.

He knew it was wrong of him to take the side of this evil

pack that included self-interest, duplicity and perfidy, and which could one day be used against him. But this did not frighten him.

His best hope, but the worst for Rovena, was to turn her into a call girl. This was the only way to dethrone the woman he loved. Otherwise, wearing her crown, and in her natural shape, as she had appeared to him one hundred years before, on the sofa after dinner in Tirana, Rovena was impossible to deal with. The years had not diminished her but only made her more dangerous.

This new mask, tawdry as it was, was his last hope, and behind it there remained only . . . only . . . What was it that lay behind the mask and its tawdriness? Perhaps a loss of lustre, a wiping away of steam from the face of the mirror, like an erasure, which itself was a form of escape, and so on, until one reached the bare and brutal thought of something . . . that resembled murder. He was astonished at the appearance of this tempta- tion. It arrived suddenly, quietly, hovering as if above some barren plateau in his mind. There it took shape, inert and motionless, unconnected to measurable time. He thought less of the murder itself than of the ease of committing it. A murder was not difficult in Europe, and was easier in Albania than anywhere else. Everywhere there were little motels, which no one ever noticed, where every trace could be obliterated for two thousand euros.

Besfort Y. shook his head, as when he wanted to shake off a nasty thought.

It couldn't be true, he said to himself. These thoughts were like the images of sleep that came and went for no cause or reason.

He imagined Rovena dozing, her knees drawn up on the seat in her train carriage, which could as well be the sofa that evening in Tirana, and he longed for her.

The drunk had followed him. Besfort felt his breath before he heard his voice. "These signs with the wrong mileage, and the wrong directions, you don't need to speak the language to understand them."

Besfort turned his back to him.

He felt tired and numbed by the noise of the train. The turning wheels beat out Rovena's pitilessly repeated question: why was he doing this? What was he looking for? He was surely looking for something impossible. Just like him . . . the dictator . . . He was looking for the love of traitors.

The monster, he thought. How could he infect us with this disease?

Chapter Eight

Twelve weeks before. The other zone.
Three chapters from Don Quixote.

He was the first to call it "the other zone". Then they both used the phrase as naturally as if it were the eurozone or the Schengen area.

He sent her the plane ticket to come to Albania with a brief note. "This time you'll see your family. I think this will suit. I really am curious. B."

He looked lingeringly at the word "curious", as if it were of archaeological interest, like a stone inscription. Under it lay another stratum, with his earlier phrase, "I really am . . . missing you" now cruelly buried.

She replied in the same style. "Thanks for the ticket. I'm very curious too. R."

Let happen what may. Just let me see her.

Of course both were curious. For the first time they were in that other region, where everything was different, starting with the way they talked.

In one of their few phone calls before their arrival, she had said, "How amazing that we'll do this in Tirana."

The other surprise came when he said to her that they would meet in a motel. Without giving her time to speak, he told her not to worry. This is normal in Albania nowadays.

Late in the afternoon, he collected her in his car from the street outside her house. From a distance he made out her elegant figure on the pavement and groaned inwardly, "Oh God."

As they sped along the Durrës motorway he looked at her profile out of the corner of his eye. She was white, just as he had expected. Alien, with the frozen expression of a doll, or of Japanese make-up. He had never desired her so much.

The car left the motorway to follow the road beside the beach. The lights of restaurants and hotels shone on both sides. She became animated for the first time as she read their names out loud: Hotel Monte Carlo, Bar Café Vienna, The Z Motel, The Discreet, The New Jersey, The Queen Mother's Hotel.

"This is unreal," she said. "When were all these built?"

Their hotel was set back from the road, almost in darkness among pine trees. They registered with false names. The proprietor showed them to their room. The restaurant was on the first floor. If they wished, supper could be brought to them.

The room was warm, with a burgundy carpet and provocative pictures on the walls. In the bathroom, by the side of the tub, was a bas-relief with three naked female figures.

"How amazing . . ." She said no more as she opened the curtains to look at the pine trees and the sea behind them, now

148

dim in the dusk. He leant against the bedhead watching her wander about the room like a shadow.

"Shall I get ready?"

He nodded. He felt a compression in his chest, as he lay in a trance of happiness. How would she "get ready" this time? Differently from before, he was sure . . .

The lamps glowed softly. His heartbeat slowed as he imagined her undressing. Of course it would be different from before, and she would take longer to prepare herself.

He thought that she would never come out. How long she's taking, he thought. He could no longer hear the slight noises to which his ears had been accustomed for years.

He got up from the bed and slowly moved to the bathroom, as if sleepwalking. The door was half open. He pushed it and entered. "Rovena," hc said aloud. She was not there.

Her toiletries, comb, perfume bottle, lipstick were all there, beneath the mirror. A pair of silk panties lay beside the bath, delicate, pale blue, as if part of the porcelain decoration. "Rovena," he said again, faintly now. How could she have vanished like this? Unnoticed, without even a creak of the door.

He looked at her things again in the mirror, and at his own face, now grown unfamiliar. She was yours and you lost her, he said to himself reproachfully. You let her slip though your fingers.

He turned abruptly, thinking she had suddenly appeared. But it was not Rovena herself. It was her image. One of the figures on the bas-relief strangely resembled her. How had he failed to notice this? So there's the plaster you wanted, he said to himself.

It was no mere simulacrum. This was Rovena herself. Apparently, she had found her form and taken shelter in it. That was her very neck, her breasts, her marble belly, all distant, on the other side, just as in his folly he had dreamed. Crazy, he said to himself. Lunatic.

He sat on the side of the bath and held his head in his hands. He wanted to weep. Nothing like this had ever happened before. He thought he would sit there for ever, until he felt a hand touch his hair. He didn't open his eyes, terrified of seeing the marble arm stretching out from the bas-relief and stroking him. He heard her voice, "Besfort, are you asleep?" and he shivered.

She was standing beside the bed, with the white hotel bathrobe half open about her.

"I don't know what happened to me," he said. "I dozed off."

Here were the same breasts, the same marble waist that he had seen a few moments ago as he slept.

He drew her to him hurriedly and eagerly, as if to prove that this was warm flesh and blood, and she responded. Her neck and armpits were warm and soft, but her lips were still imprisoned in the marble. Fiercely, like a storm accompanied by claps of thunder, their lips brushed against each other, but without daring to violate the eternal pact between a whore and her client: no kissing.

He kissed her belly and groaned as he moved lower, to the dark cavern, where the rules were different and so was the pact.

As his panting subsided, without waiting for the usual question, how was it?, she said softly into his ear, "Heavenly."

He stroked her hair.

Outside, darkness must have fallen.

He suggested a walk beside the sea before dinner. The darkness was sinister. The iron railings round the villas stood black and forlorn.

She leant against his shoulder, their conversation barely audible against the booming of the waves. She asked if those pale lights in the distance were from King Zog's villa. Besfort thought they might be. The heir to the throne and his court had recently returned to Albania, along with Queen Geraldine. The newspapers reported that she was close to death.

"Incredible," she said after a pause. He wanted to know what she found incredible, and she tried to answer, but her words were partly obliterated by the sound of the sea. The restaurants along the road with their Hollywood names were incredible, and so were the villas with their private swimming pools, the former communists turning into oligarchs, the former middle classes turning into God knows what and the glimmering lights of the Royal Court with their tug of nostalgia.

For some reason she wanted to burst into tears. Besfort and his madness were stranger than all these things – and so was she herself as she followed him through that darkness.

They could hardly find their way back. Don't turn down your coat collar, he said, when they were close to the motel. She wanted to ask why, but remembered the false names and said nothing. They ordered supper in their room. There were all kinds of specialities and expensive wines on the menu. The proprietor recommended game, just delivered, and Italian Gaja wine, the prime minister's favourite. A likely story, said Besfort. But he made no objection.

When they were left alone, their eyes met tenderly. Usually after a glance of this sort, she would say, "How happy I am with you!" He waited to hear the words, but saw her hesitate. He bowed his head.

Really, nothing was the same as before.

She said something else he could not catch, as if it were in a strange language. "What?" he asked softly. She asked him if she should get changed, wear something more, you know, stylish, for supper.

"Of course," he replied. Just like a call girl, he thought.

Her black velvet dress accentuated the unbearable whiteness of her décolletage and the exposed sides of her breasts that drove him to distraction. He could not believe that he had slept with her hundreds of times. Or just two hours before.

"Just now, when we were by the sea, we saw the lights of Zog's villa and I remembered what you told me last time about the bogus conspirators."

"Really?"

"Don't be so surprised. I never forget anything you tell me." She touched her forehead, as people do when making fun of themselves. "I kept thinking of what you said during those three weeks when I was writing the part of my dissertation about the conspiracies against King Zog."

"And what were those conspiracies like?"

Finally she laughed. There were pale crimson patches on her cheeks and neck from the wine.

"At least they were real."

"I'm sure they were. But you'll tell me later, won't you."

From the way they looked at each other, they seemed to be thinking the same thing. That at least the hour after midnight would be the same as before.

"You'll tell me about the plots against the king, and I'll tell you something else."

"Really?" she said. "What fun!"

"Goddess, tell me about the plots against the king, the real ones."

"We didn't give real names at the reception," said Rovena teasingly.

He did not reply. His expression was stony.

She cast playful glances at him, but his face in profile became even more rigid.

"Do you remember the first time we went to the Loreley?" he asked suddenly, coming round.

"The singles club? What made you think of that now?" said Rovena. "That must be four or five years ago."

He laughed.

"More like four or five centuries."

With a relaxed smile, she waited for him to sit down beside her again. He held in his hand a small book bound in burgundy.

"Four or five centuries? Did you really mean that?"

"That's what I said." Besfort took a deep breath. "Do you remember when we opened the door to the Loreley. I don't think we were the first couple to feel shocked. It was the fear of breaking a taboo."

He would never forget that late afternoon when, both hiding their nervousness, they got ready to go there. As they moved round the room, they lowered their voices.

The most hurtful pang was to see her lengthy preparations in the bathroom. He watched her through the half-open door: her concentration in front of the mirror, touching up her eyelashes, giving some last attention to her underarms. This was the first time he had seen her getting ready not just for him, but for all the male sex.

"Of course I remember," she replied.

Besfort gave her a penetrating look. "Everybody thinks this is a new, modern experience, but it's been well known down the ages. At least it was described four or five centuries ago in this story."

Rovena read aloud the title of the little book: "Miguel Cervantes, *The Tale of the Foolish Test of Virtue*. This is part of *Don Quixote*, isn't it?"

"Exactly. Long before he produced his full translation, Fan Noli published this extract, to whet his readers' appetites. No doubt about it, this describes an early version of a modern singles club."

"How extraordinary," she said.

"And to think that Noli was a long-faced bishop of Albania. And a conspirator, I think. You will know more about it."

"Not just a conspirator, but the absolute linchpin. He was involved in at least three plots."

"It's an uncanny story," Besfort went on.

He had made notes in the margin while reading, as if inter-preting an occult text.

She was leafing though it with curiosity, but Besfort gently took it out of her hands.

"You can have a look at it after supper."

He raised his glass.

"The wine is delicious, but I think I've drunk enough," Rovena said.

Her cheeks bore the blush that naturally brings love to mind. At the entrance to the Loreley her face had been pale. He now knew for certain that she was attracted to the prospect of trans-gression, avoid it as she might.

"I'll take a shower," said Besfort. "You've got time to look through that little book, if you like."

"I certainly will," she said. "I can hardly wait."

Chapter Nine

The same night. A Cervantes text.

Under the jet of hot water, Besfort tried to imagine what Rovena would make of the medieval Spanish city and the two inseparable friends, Lothario and Anselmo. And the sweet Camilla, the latter's bride who unwittingly becomes the reason why Lothario cools slightly towards his bosom friend. The newlyweds notice this coldness and it worries them.

Besfort imagined Rovena's tapered fingers turning the pages.

So the young couple are concerned. They encourage their friend to come to them as before, and to make their home his own. Lothario visits, but nervously. He is scared of rumours. But the couple are not worried about these at all. The shadow of anxiety that Lothario sometimes sees cross his friend's brow has a quite different cause. One day Anselmo opens his heart. He is gnawed by an obsession, one that might drive him mad. Of course he is happy with his bride, but he cannot allay this pain. It involves a suspicion. Lothario should not stare like that. This suspicion is about nothing less than Camilla's constancy.

Besfort knew that Rovena's delicate fingers would turn the pages eagerly.

Wait, Anselmo says to his friend, not letting him speak. He knows what he's going to say. He also knows that his Camilla is spotlessly pure. But ... can a woman be called virtuous if she has never had the chance to be wicked?

Besfort imagined Rovena's eyebrows and lashes, so carefully made up, trembling like a swallow's wings at an approaching storm.

Lothario does all he can to reassure his friend. But there is no cure for his obsession. As if tormented by a fever, he reverts again and again to his dark suspicions. Finally, he makes a grotesque suggestion. Only Lothario, his faithful friend, can free him from this nightmare. There is only one way to prove Camilla's constancy; he admits it is a dangerous game, but it is foolproof. Lothario must put Camilla to the test, in short, seduce her. Trap her.

Besfort imagined Rovena's nervous fingers turning back the pages to reread them, the steady glow on her cheeks matching the ruby in her ring.

Lothario rejects the suggestion with contempt. He takes serious offence. He gets up to leave. For ever. But a single utterance from Anselmo stops him in his tracks. It is a threat. If Lothario will not do it, he will find a total stranger. Some ordinary lecher. Some low rat.

Lothario holds his head in his hands. This threat crushes his resistance. He takes on this appalling task, or rather pretends to. He decides to deceive his friend, as one might humour a lunatic.

And so, when the hour of trial comes, sitting opposite Camilla, he does not make the slightest move. Anselmo can barely wait to hear the outcome. Lothario tells him: Camilla is as pure as crystal, as white as mountain snow. She called him a swine. She repulsed his advances. She threatened to tell her husband.

But Anselmo does not believe what he hears. His expression darkens. "Traitor!" he says. "Double-crosser! I watched you through the keyhole. You're telling lies. You sat there like a poker. Scumbag! What kind of a seducer are you? Now you'll see, I'll bring in the real libertines. The real fornicators. At least they don't lie."

Lothario tries to calm him down. He begs forgiveness. He asks for another chance. A test of loyalty. One last time. Just don't bring in any lowlife.

Finally, they reach an agreement. They will both set the trap. Anselmo will go away to the country. Lothario will stay in Anselmo's home, for three days and three nights. This is Anselmo's order. Camilla makes no objection. The first evening arrives.

Besfort turned off the shower, as if to listen out for Rovena's faster breathing.

The two are alone, Lothario and Camilla. They eat dinner together, drink a little wine. They look at the fire in the hearth.

The text describes it in a few words. Lothario makes a declaration of love. Camilla desperately attempts to ward him off, but eventually her defences are exhausted. Camilla gives in. The text is pitiless, and uses the word "surrender" twice. Camilla surrenders. Camilla falls.

159

Besfort knew that Rovena would close her eyes at this point in the story. Of all the women he had known, not one shut her eyes during lovemaking in the same passionate way as Rovena. So she must have closed her eyes to imagine the scene and identify with it. Would she feel sorry that Camilla had given in? Probably the opposite, she would hardly be able to wait . . .

At the brightly lit entrance to the Loreley, Besfort put more or less the same question for the umpteenth time. Was she enjoying this? Rovena's wan face gave no answer.

Finally, they entered and began to explore the club's premises. Rovena was totally naked apart from the scanty underwear that the rules demanded. He wore even less. And so they wandered though the dim rooms, until they came to a huge bed. Here they sat down to collect themselves. As their eyes grew used to the gloom, they recovered from their shock enough to discern what was happening around them. There were beds here and there, some occupied. On one, a couple was making love. Other people roamed about. There were women wearing only lingerie, sometimes nothing at all. Men in briefs. Single men wandering like ghosts. Someone was carrying a drink to his girlfriend. Everything was calm and harmonious.

"You have the most beautiful breasts of anybody here," he whispered. There was a gleam in Rovena's eye that discouraged speech. He said it a second time. "Not just breasts either," he added.

Her thigh was bent at an angle, and part of the dark region between her legs was visible. At this very spot, at the narrow opening in her underwear, one of the men stared with longing.

"Everybody fancies you," Besfort whispered.

"Really?"

"And that little part that doesn't seem special to you is driving that guy crazy."

"I can see that," she said. But still she did not make the slightest move to cover it.

"In ancient times, I forget where, people used to have sex in public places," Besfort said.

"Really?"

"There was nothing cheap about it, it was a serious thing, in fact almost a sacred ritual, like celebrations nowadays." She grasped his hand. "What about us? Here?" he asked.

She nodded. "Wait a bit. I haven't got used to the place yet." Suddenly, she shivered and drew in her leg. A man with gentle eyes had bent down to touch her ankle.

"Don't be frightened," said Besfort. The man eyed her tenderly with a guilty, long-suffering look. "I think that's a sign," Besfort said. "He wants permission to make love to you."

She bit her fingers.

Everywhere around them was the same cult-like atmosphere. "Shall we look around?" she said. They stood up, and she took him by the hand. It seemed natural to him that she should lead him, like Virgil, he thought. As they walked, a door marked "Massage" caught their eyes . . .

Besfort finished his shower. Rovena must almost have finished the story.

Anselmo comes back from the country to learn the outcome. Lothario of course tells him the opposite of what really happened. Anselmo seems content. The test of constancy is over. Lothario now comes and goes, treating Anselmo's house as his own. Deception has triumphed. Everything is topsy-turvy. The more Camilla's honour is praised to the skies, the deeper she sinks into the mire, as Lothario does too. Then events rush pell-mell to catastrophe. One night, just before dawn, Lothario, blinded by jealousy, sees a strange man coming out of Anselmo's house. He instantly thinks it is Camilla's new lover. Lecher, scumbag, fornicator! These words of Anselmo's now come to his own mind, but with a new meaning.

Besfort always thought the story ended here. He had never paid much attention to its coda, Lothario's rage against Camilla, his desire for revenge, the confusion with the servant girl, the escape of the guilty pair, the scandal and finally the death of all three, one driven mad, one speared in a battle and one pining in a convent.

As he dried his hair, he thought that Rovena must have raced through the last pages as he had done.

He slowly opened the bathroom door and saw her stretched on her back, staring abstractedly at the ceiling. The book lay open beside her.

Their eyes finally met. Her own were vacant, as if any anger she might have felt had already ebbed away. Besfort expected a vigorous reaction, but their conversation was awkward. Finally she asked him why he had given her this little book.

He shrugged his shoulders. "Why? For no particular reason."

"Besfort, you don't often do things without a reason."

"OK, let's say I have a reason. What harm was there in it?

What do you think was at the back of my mind?" Rovena did not answer. Besfort said he was sure she had read it before. *Don Quixote*? Of course. At high school, it was a set text. Fighting the windmills. Dulcinea del Toboso. But she scarcely remembered this part at all.

"Besfort, tell me the truth. You gave me this to read because you think it somehow relates to ourselves, I mean to both of us."

"Somehow relates to us?" Besfort laughed. "Not somehow, but totally. And not just to us, but to everybody." He stroked her hair as she lay down beside him. In words that came to him with difficulty, he explained that this story was in a way archetypal. It described a sort of infernal machine through which millions of couples passed, consciously or otherwise.

Rovena struggled to follow his meaning. So it was an occult text that needed a key to unlock it.

"Don't look at me like that, as if I were sick," he said.

Gently she touched his hand.

He said he had always liked it when she looked like a sympathetic nurse. It was no accident that nurses made such tender lovers. But he wasn't crazy, as she might think.

Rovena stroked his hand. Of course he didn't seem crazy to her. If anybody was crazy, then they both were. Or had been at one time.

"You mean at the Loreley," he butted in.

They recalled their visit there, without pretending they hadn't been thinking of the tale of the foolish test of virtue. The two stories were essentially so close that they almost coincided, and the phrase "infernal machine" was not accidental either. Both stories brought to mind the afterworld, not the familiar hell with its tortures and fiery cauldrons, but another gentler, muted, pre-Christian kind.

How bewildered they had been at first as they wandered through the dim spaces, until the huge bed loomed in front of them like some rock of salvation. Their second expedition took them to the bar in search of drinks, and then further afield. She grew more relaxed as she walked, her silk-sheathed hips swayed more freely, until they came to the door marked "Massage".

Would you like that? he asked her, with his eyes rather than in words. She barely hesitated. If he didn't mind.

The door closed behind her and he turned back to find a place to wait for her. From a distance, he saw the bed where they had lain, still vacant. He sat down on it and lay back on one elbow, a solitary Ulysses cast up by the waves, surrounded by the booming of the sea. Around him, the ebb and flow continued. A couple paused beside him and started talking to each other. The woman stepped forward, bent down, touched his ankle. Besfort produced a guilty smile. He wanted to explain that this lady was very attractive and classy, but he had something else on his mind. He whispered, "I'm sorry," but the two lowered their heads to say goodbye so politely that he was sincerely touched to the heart. He watched them move away arm-in-arm, but could not muster the willpower to stand up and follow them. He wanted to tell them how much he would have liked to stay with them, with this noble lady and this gentleman, sharing their sophisticated ennui on this bed where destiny had landed them. He felt genuinely sad, but for a different reason. Sometimes he thought of Rovena, and sometimes he put her behind him. She seemed to him light years away, sucked away by a whirling universe resembling one of the dormant galaxies captured in the latest space photos. The fear that she would never return came so naturally to him that he reflected he should not complain, because they had spent so many wonderful years together. He would do better to find out where this debilitating numbness came from. It was as if he had been smoking hashish. Perhaps it was the stress of this exhausting day, or was it time to take that Doppler test, as his doctor was insisting?

The languid crowd still circulated. A woman with tearful eyes and a tulip in her hand appeared to be looking for someone. He would not have been surprised to see, among the milling swarm, people he knew from the Council of Europe – those who had first given him the club's address. Rovena was taking a long time. The tear-stained woman passed by again. Instead of the tulip she held a document of some kind in her hand. She was looking for somebody. Besfort thought that if she came a little closer he would surely distinguish on the document the initials and seal of the ICTY. The International Criminal Tribunal at The Hague.

A court summons! Rubbish, he thought. Go and wave that scrap of paper in front of someone else! Yet he averted his head in order not to meet her eyes.

He dozed off two or three times, until Rovena finally reappeared, as if emerging out of a fog, or arriving from dozens or thousands of light years away. Of course she would be changed. The whites of her eyes had a devastating gleam. There were vacant spaces in them. Her words were also sparse.

"When I came back you were in a trance," said Rovena. "I expected you to ask me what it was like."

"I don't know what was stopping me," he said. "Maybe I thought you wouldn't be able to tell the truth even if you wanted to."

"Perhaps," she replied. "Sometimes that really does happen."

He took a deep breath.

"It's what usually happens. And it is a really peculiar thing that love, the most beautiful emotion on earth, is the one least able to bear the truth."

"I don't know what to say," she said.

"It's different now. You're free now. We're both different now. Do you see what I mean? We're both entirely different, so now you can say it."

She remained silent, but she took his hand that was stroking her stomach into her own, and guided it where she wanted.

"Do you really want to know?" she said in a lifeless voice. Did he really want to know, after so long? The words of both of them, broken by their laboured breathing, died out into silence.

"Now I understand why you gave me the Cervantes text," said Rovena when they were calm again.

He had not worked it out so precisely, he said. He had been drawn to the text first out of curiosity and its resemblance to the Loreley. The other things came later.

"You told me the text contained a mystery, and that you had found the key to its meaning."

"I don't think I'm the only one. Would you like to hear about it? Aren't you tired?"

"Don't back out," she said. "You told me that the hour after midnight would be the same as it has always been."

"That's true. I promised."

She took a deep breath.

"The hour when a prostitute tells her interested client about her orphaned childhood, drunken father, insane mother."

"That's enough," he interrupted, clapping his hand over her mouth. He felt her lips under his palm, gently squeezed into a kiss, and his heart leaped.

Chapter Ten

That same night. The occult text.

Slowly he began to explain his interpretation of the text. Rarely had such a great deception been portrayed in such a covert manner. Treachery triumphed. All the characters were waiting their turn to deceive or be deceived. Camilla, the young bride, is first deceived by Anselmo, her own husband who puts her to the test, and then by Lothario, their house guest, who agrees to play the game. Then Lothario, now Camilla's lover, deceives her again by failing to confess to her how the story started.

Anselmo, with his mania for putting his wife to the test, is deceived by both Camilla and Lothario, who become lovers behind his back.

Truth is violated to such an extent that when Lothario acts honestly he is vilified for treachery, and when he becomes a deceiver he is revered as a saint. The same goes for Camilla. First she is suspected of being inconstant when she is not, and then she is praised for her sanctity when she yields.

"The only character in the story who deceives without being deceived is Lothario. Do you agree with that?"

Rovena did not know what to say.

"Or so it seems," continued Besfort. "But probably the opposite is true. In all likelihood, he is the only one who is a victim of deceit."

He went on to explain that the most mysterious passage in the tale describes the morning before dawn when Lothario sees a stranger coming out of Anselmo's house. Lothario jumps to the conclusion that Camilla has a lover. Did she find him herself? Or did Anselmo plant him there, to repeat his test? Curiously, Cervantes suggests only the first possibility. He does not raise the second at all, although it is just as likely, if not more so.

Any careful reader must ask a serious question. What is Lothario doing outside Anselmo's house before dawn? Why is he on the lookout? What does he suspect?

This question turns the entire text inside out, and here is the new interpretation.

Anselmo and Camilla, after they are engaged or married, discover the miracle of sex. Their passion for each other is such that they turn the marital bed, so often derided as a desert of tedium, into an altar to the boundlessness of desire. With the passage of time their lusts become ever more refined, pushing them towards an ultimate liberation. They try every kind of sex they have ever heard of or imagined. They talk dirty, they perform the most shameful acts. They know no limits. As they eat dinner with friends and go to market or Sunday mass, they think of nothing but the hour after dinner, when she comes

170

with a candle in her hand to the bed where he is waiting for her, his desire hotter than the melting wax. In sombre, mighty Spain, bristling with cathedrals, with its protocols of the Inquisition and its spies, these two are set apart. They discover a kind of passion that few have ever known, which transports them every night to unknown regions. The barriers of shame fall one after another, and the couple break through inhibitions and taboos, until one day they stand before the gateway of decision. "Would you like to try it with someone else?" A long silence. Then the answer, "Why not?" And then the question, "What about you?" and silence again. And then the reply, "To tell the truth, yes."

And so, trembling with terror and lust, they embark on the great trial. Everything about it is unnerving. Especially the selection of their partner and victim. First they suggest Lothario, but they both reject this choice as too reckless. He is too close a friend. They think of others, but they are no good either. The first is bald, the second has some other flaw, the third isn't serious and the fourth not man enough. Camilla notices with delight that her husband is not deviously choosing someone lesser than himself. This makes it easier for them to come back to Lothario. Camilla says candidly that he fits the bill. Anselmo makes no objection. He suits them both. In short, he excites them both.

And so events take their course. But the difference is that Anselmo never leaves the house. Excitedly, he watches Camilla making herself ready for another man. He senses her impatience, which matches his own. Then, from the place where he hides, with Camilla's knowledge, he observes everything: Lothario's declaration of love, Camilla's bowed head. He watches them draw close and kiss for the first time. Then from another vantage point he watches them go to the bed and undress. He hears Camilla's familiar cry, and sees her pale legs carelessly splayed after their lovemaking. He can hardly wait for the other man to leave, so that he can make love to his wife.

And so it goes on for several weeks, or perhaps months, until the day of the catastrophe. There is no doubt that a disaster occurs, and it is entirely credible that Lothario, now in the role of eavesdropper, should see someone leaving the house in secret. What is not credible in the story as Cervantes tells it is the introduction of the servant girl's love affair, and so on. In fact, it is not the servant girl's lover leaving the house, but Camilla's.

And this is what the new reading tells us really happened:

Camilla and Anselmo quickly tire of Lothario, and want to stretch their limits again. As is usual in such cases, they want fresh stimulus. And so they need a new partner, as Anselmo had predicted they would from the start.

Lothario has noticed something odd. His suspicions have been aroused. That is why he spies on his friend's house every night until he discovers the truth.

Here the curtain falls on the drama and we are left in darkness. Something serious happens, something that brings death to all three, but for some reason this is not revealed.

Besfort was tired, and he fell silent. As so often when he spoke again after an interval, his eyelids moved first.

"A strange story," said Rovena, with averted eyes. "Do you want to know what happened in the Loreley?" she added.

He paused before replying.

"I didn't tell you the story with that in mind, believe me."

"I do believe you. But I want you to know."

He felt the familiar stab in his heart.

She spoke with her eyes lifted, as if telling her story to the ceiling.

"I wasn't unfaithful to you in the Loreley," she said calmly.

Each avoided the other's eyes. In a steady voice, as if talking about someone else, Rovena described what had happened. Besfort listened with the same detachment, reflecting with sorrow that there is a proper time to ask every question, and he was no longer curious about the Loreley. She had walked to the massage couch, and the masseur was "suitable", as she and Besfort would have described him, like Camilla and Anselmo long ago . . . She described the uncertain borderline between massage and fondling, her temptation, her hesitation. With astonishing precision, she described how she cast aside all shame, but finally and unaccountably demurred on the very brink . . .

"That is all," she said. "Are you upset?"

He did not reply immediately. He cleared his throat, coughed.

"Upset? Why?"

The silence became awkward.

"Upset at what happened . . . although in fact nothing happened . . ."

"Then why should I be upset?"

She felt an emptiness in the pit of her stomach.

"I could ask it differently. Are you upset because nothing happened?"

"No," he said curtly. "Not for that reason either."

Suddenly, Rovena felt traduced. The old question of where she had made a mistake surfaced again, accompanied by all the anxieties she thought she had left behind. As people so often do, in trying to repair her blunder she merely made it worse.

"Don't you even care?" she cried despairingly.

She was on the verge of breaking down in tears.

"Listen, Rovena," he said calmly. "I don't know how to talk to you. Until yesterday you were complaining that it was my fault that you aren't free. And now you say you have too much freedom. But somehow it's always my fault."

"I'm sorry," she butted in. "I know, I know. Please forgive me. We're different now. We have a pact. You're the client, I'm the prost ... The call girl. I don't have the right ... I ..."

"That's enough," he said. "There's no need for a drama. There's enough of that around."

Years ago he had shouted "That's enough" in just the same way. Ashen-faced and with a trembling hand, he had grabbed her by the hair, just by the window, and the appalling thought flashed through her mind, oh my God, here I am being treated like a whore in the middle of Europe.

He did not hit her. With a pale stare, as if he himself had been struck, he sank onto the sofa.

It was all over. The thought came to her, that of the two "enoughs" she would have chosen the first, and she burst into a torrent of tears. Tyrant, she said to herself. You pretend you've lost your power, but you're still the same.

She heard his voice. "It's three in the morning. Shall we go to sleep?"

"Yes," she replied faintly.

They said goodnight, and a few moments later Rovena was astonished to hear his breathing deepen.

He had never before been the first to fall asleep. The emptiness of the room became somehow suspicious. This is no use, she thought. You can't win against him – ever. She had lost her last chance long ago, and now it was too late. She had never resorted to her only superior weapon, her youth, because forbidden arms can never be used.

Now he was out of danger. He had persuaded her that they would come out of it together, leaving behind all their hesitations, their doubts over separating or not separating, and the question of where she had gone wrong or not gone wrong, as if these belonged to another world, like the Cervantes story, or old movies, or Greek tragedy.

Naïve as ever, she had trusted him. Now he was secure, but she was not. Not at all. His steady, pitiless breathing testified to his domination.

Tyrant, she said to herself again. Just before you were overthrown, you voluntarily gave up the crown. "I'm abdicating. I myself am standing down," you said. "Nobody will ever topple me."

Do what you want, take power or reject it. There is no way I can escape from you, not even from your shadow, or from your dust as you fall. I have been yours. I accept your rule and I am not ashamed. I don't want that crown myself, because I want something else – to be a woman. Totally a woman. To suffer, and if I want to dominate, to do so through suffering.

A woman, she repeated to herself.

Sleep eluded her. Slowly she got out of bed and went to his bedside table. There, next to his glass of water, was a small packet of sedatives. *Stilnox*, she read. Quiet night.

She picked up the packet with a kind of tenderness. Here was his balm. These were what calmed his mind.

As she stretched her hand to the water glass, her eyes fell on a black object. Inside the half-open drawer was a revolver.

She caught her breath. She remembered all at once the secrecy of this journey, the false names at the reception desk and his advice to her to turn up the collar of her coat. What was it all about? But then she recalled him saying that he always travelled armed in Albania, and she calmed down at once.

Without further ado, she detached a tablet from the blister pack and swallowed it.

In bed, she lay back and waited for sleep. How had she been reduced to this? She didn't even have the right to call him "darling".

She tried not to think any more. Perhaps she was demanding more of this world than she should. A woman like her didn't need much.

Sleep would come soon. She was curious to know what kind of oblivion his sedative would bring, as if the nature of his sleep would reveal more of his secrets.

But perhaps she didn't even need to know his secrets. A woman like her needed to know only one thing, that there had been nights when Besfort Y. had taken these sleeping pills because of her . . . That was sufficient.

As she listened to his deep breathing, she thought that this sedative had finally helped her enter his brain. Now, however clever he was, he could not hide.

His breathing was changing, but she would stay vigilant. Now it was her turn to trick him by pretending to be asleep.

Apparently Besfort had been waiting for this moment. He moved slowly, not to waken her. Then he reached out to the drawer beside the bed. Is he in his right mind? she thought.

It was obvious what he was doing. She had no reason to pretend she didn't understand. She heard the scrape of the drawer and the movement of his hand as he took out the gun. Oh God, she prayed. She had feared being killed in a motel, and now it was happening. But instead of acting to save herself, she remembered a whores' song:

> If she doesn't end up in a ditch,
> In a Golem motel you'll find this bitch.

The cold barrel of the gun touched her ribs just below the right breast. In spite of the silencer, she heard the trigger and felt the bullet enter her flesh.

So this is what he wanted, she thought.

She saw his arm make the same circular motion to replace the weapon. Then there was silence. How incredible, she thought. He had fallen asleep straight after the crime, in the same position, lying on his side.

Rovena pressed her hand to the wound to staunch the blood. Besfort was breathing deeply again. Had this struggle worn him out so much? thought Rovena, as if treating him with indulgence for the last time.

She stood up and moved silently to the bathroom. The wound held no terror for her. It looked clean, almost as if drawn by hand. Among her cosmetics under the mirror she found a sticking plaster of the kind she usually kept with her. She fixed it to the wound and felt reassured at once. At least she would not give up the ghost like some motel whore.

Incredible, she thought again, climbing back into bed. He was still sleeping as if nothing had happened. Just like one thousand years ago, she lay down beside him.

Chapter Eleven

The next day. Morning.

He had no right to behave like this. She spent most of her mornings alone, and he should have been beside her on this one. Even before she opened her eyes, her bare arm groped for him, but he wasn't there. Drowsily, she stretched her arm further, to the edge of the bed. Beyond lay Austria and the plains of Europe. The names of great cities glowed palely like on old wireless sets, fraught with terror. He shouldn't do this. Inevitably he would be the first to go, leaving her alone in this world for many long years. So he shouldn't be in a hurry now.

Finally she opened her eyes. The waking world was in order. It was simple and obvious: he had gone for a walk through the pine trees while waiting for her to wake up. Scraps of daylight filtered awkwardly through the shutters. The little burgundy Cervantes lay there inert, weary of its old secret.

She heard steps and the door handle turned. He bent down to kiss her temple. He was carrying the morning papers. Over breakfast, he glanced through the headlines.

"The queen is ill," Rovena said.

He said nothing.

She set aside her coffee cup and phoned home. "Mother, I'm in Durrës with my girlfriends. Don't be worried."

The coffee struck Besfort as particularly good. How sweet this world could be, with queens ill and women telling white lies.

"Look at this," Rovena said, handing him a newspaper.

Besfort laughed, and read aloud, "'Baroness Fatime Gurthi, spokesperson of the Tirana Water Board, attempted to justify the water shortage.' Buying titles is the latest fashion. A thousand dollars, and you wake up a count or a marquis."

"I thought it was a joke, but even in jest it makes no sense."

Besfort replied that it was no joke. There were international agencies that trafficked titles. Everybody in the former East was crazy about them.

"That's all we need," said Rovena.

Besfort was sure he had the business card of a certain Viscount Shabë Dulaku (Reinforced Doors and Windows Made To Order) from the suburb of Lapraka. He'd heard of a duke in the traffic police and a countess who had written a booklet entitled *Albanian Irregular Verbs*.

After breakfast they went out for a walk along the shore. A fierce wind blew, and it seemed an alien, indifferent kind of day. Clinging tightly to his arm, Rovena felt her hair strike Besfort's face.

She did not know whether she was still supposed to tell him everything that was on her mind or not. She had the impression that the eyes of both of them had become as hard as glass in the wind. Even if she wanted to, she wouldn't be able to admit everything, not even to herself.

Behind iron railings, the swimming pools were frozen. Films of ice like cataracts spread over the surface of the water.

They found a restaurant for lunch and then spent the whole afternoon locked in their room. In bed, before they made love, he caressed her and whispered something about Liza. He had forgotten all the little details, or pretended to have done. She replied to him in the same whisper. He told her that nobody understood men like she did. Rovena flattered him in the same way.

As dusk fell Rovena spoke to her mother again on the phone while Besfort switched on the television to see if there was news of the Queen. "It's lovely here, Mother. We're going to stay tonight too."

As she spoke, he stroked her belly, tracing circles around her navel.

Evening deepened fast. As midnight approached, the roaring of the sea sounded increasingly plangent. In the morning they left the hotel in a hurry, not knowing themselves why they felt so flustered. As they drove towards Tirana, the traffic grew heavier. There seemed to be more florists than ever at the cross-roads leading to the western cemetery. We all get flowers sooner or later, thought Rovena. She remembered scraps of their conversation about the bogus conspirators. Some of them must be buried here. They would have flowers like everybody else.

At the entrance to Tirana the line of vehicles was barely

moving. A traffic policeman walked past their car and Besfort asked him if there had been an accident. The policeman glanced at their licence plate out of the corner of his eye before he answered.

"The queen is dead," he said.

Besfort switched on the radio and they heard the queen mentioned. But the voices were raised in anger. They were arguing. By the time they reached Kavaja Street it became clear what it was all about: the funeral ceremony and also the site of her grave. The government, as always, was caught on the wrong foot.

"Just wait, they'll appeal to some commission in Brussels next," said Rovena.

Near Skenderbeg Square they heard a statement from the Royal Court. A requiem for the queen would be sung at St. Paul's Cathedral at three o'clock that afternoon. No word about the burial site. The government had still not issued a ruling about the restitution of the king's property, including the family graves, in the south-east of the capital.

They had almost reached Rovena's house when the radio broadcast a second statement from the court. The place of burial was still undecided.

"This is scandalous," Rovena said, opening the car door.

On his way back, Besfort wanted to take the street past the cathedral, but it was cordoned off. After an announcement that the parliament would convene for an emergency session early in the afternoon, the radio carried interviews with ordinary passers-by. "This is a disgrace, a total disgrace," said one anonymous citizen. "To begrudge a patch of land for the queen's grave, it's crazy." – "And you, sir?" – "I don't know much about these things. I think we should follow the law. The law should hold good for the wife of the king or the president as for everybody else." – "Are you alluding to the dictator's widow?" – "What? No, no. Don't get me mixed up in that sort of thing. I was talking about the queen and other serious issues, not about that old witch."

The radio interrupted the interviews to announce that a third statement from the Royal Court was imminent.

Chapter Twelve

The Hague. The last forty days.

For a long time there was no evidence that Besfort Y., and still less both of them, had been in The Hague forty days before the end of the story. In fact, indications that they were in Denmark on that day seemed to eliminate the slightest suspicion of such a thing. Rovena's friend in Switzerland, usually cautious in her testimony, was certain of it: Rovena had phoned from the train just after crossing the Danish border. Jottings in Rovena's notebook, made four days before, supplied further evidence of her intended journey. "Jutland. Saxo Grammaticus. Villages where the events of *Hamlet* (Amleth) took place . . . Two-day visit."

In fact, suspicions regarding The Hague had taken root immediately after the reported exclamation "I'll see you both in The Hague", uttered by Rovena's intimate friend Liza.

There was no supporting evidence for a visit to The Hague from travel tickets or hotel registrations. The convincing alibi of Denmark also nearly banished this suspicion as quickly as it had arisen. This trip was like one of those imaginary journeys that take place in the minds of would-be travellers, or, in the case of The Hague, in the minds of those who are keen to see someone in the dock. However, a few lines in the diary of Janek B., Rovena's Slovak classmate and casual lover, mentioned again the fateful destination of The Hague. In this diary was a brief and obscure description of a nightmare in which the dreamer saw pieces of white paper announcing apartments for sale stuck on telephone poles, but from a distance looking like a summons to the Hague Tribunal.

The discovery of another diary notebook put an end to the confusion by making sense of the writer's style and casting light on both the relationship between the Slovak and the beautiful Albanian and the matter of the nightmare, which was not the Slovak student's, but Besfort's.

"After that unexpectedly generous night, R. changed," wrote Janek B. In a few terse words he described his pain, although he avoided using the word "pain" itself, and particularly that other word, "suffering".

His notes were vague, with phrases often left incomplete, but they still conveyed the distress he had felt the following evening when Rovena had failed to keep her appointment at the bar.

He drank. He tried not to show how he felt in front of others. A few days previously he had said half-jokingly, "We from the East have had our share of suffering. Let us not suffer in love too. Now it's the turn of you Westerners."

He thought he saw the retort in the eyes of one of his friends, "My dear Janek, there is suffering under any regime."

Rovena was different when she came to the university the next day. She explained that someone had arrived from her own country, Albania. Her face was pale, and in her nervous haste she could not concentrate. A mafia type? A trafficker in women? A lover? Janek B. made three guesses about this mysterious visitor. Which was most likely? The newspapers were full of reports of Albanian gangsters. They arrived from their distant country, made threats and then vanished, leaving emptiness and terror behind them.

Janek B. had tactfully broached the subject with Rovena, but she had blinked and failed to understand him. When she had grasped what he was on about, she said no, he had nothing to do with things like that, not with ... trafficking ... threats ...

He wanted to shake her by the shoulders and ask: "What the hell is the matter with you?" But something stopped him. "R. in the bar this evening again. But it's no go now." They sat next to each other as before, under the curious gaze of the other students from the East. They were hard people to figure out. Who knows what the dictatorships did to them.

Rovena's eyes would sparkle cheerfully, only to grow dull and cloud over as she became pensive again. Did she remember that they had slept together? This question haunted Janek. He did not know how to remind her without causing offence. "Yesterday I managed to say to her: 'Do you remember that beautiful night, when we danced together for the first time and when later ...'"

The blood froze in his veins as he waited for her response.

Her eyelashes hung long and heavy. She finally looked up to say, "Yes, it was beautiful." Her voice was soft, neither cold nor tender. She could have been talking about a painting. He mentioned her visitor from far away. Who knows where the subject will lead, he thought. Rovena lowered her eyes, but the question did not seem to annoy her. Emboldened, he pressed on. "Are you always thinking about him?"

He spoke gently, almost in a whisper. When she raised her eyes, not only did she not show any trace of irritation, but her expression was full of gratitude. "How stupid of me not to realise that she didn't want to talk about anyone else," wrote Janek.

"I like complicated men," she said later, after a long silence.

"Complicated in what way?" he asked.

"In every way."

His earlier suspicions returned. Was this man mixed up in some shady business? Was he dangerous? Plenty of women fell in love with criminals. It had been quite the fashion recently.

Rovena toyed with the ends of her hair like a high-school girl in love. "He is complicated," she went on, as if talking to herself. Janek was cut to the heart to see her eyes damp with tears. "One night he cried out in his sleep because of a nightmare," she went on. Janek thought that if shouting in his sleep was the way to improve his standing in the eyes of women, he could shout to bring the house down, but he did not dare say this. He tried to look interested while Rovena told him about this man's nightmare, the famous one about the summons to The Hague stuck to telegraph poles, bus stops and trees.

"The others who saw us whispering together probably thought – thank God they've sorted themselves out."

A few days later, Janek's diary entry read: "I've made a discovery. To my shame. This shame, strangely, does not bother me. Shame is my meat and drink."

The Slovak's extraordinary realisation was that the mysterious visitor, who he thought had robbed him of Rovena, was in fact now bringing her closer to him.

He had acquiesced in what many would call a serious humiliation. He was going out with a woman on condition that he talked about another man!

This condition was of course never made explicit, but he was aware of it. Rovena was obviously impatient as they skimmed through other topics in order to reach "him". She admitted candidly that they had been together for years. She described their trips together, their hotels, beaches in winter. She never said that they were now facing a crisis, but this too was apparent.

"It's incredible what has happened! We slept together again," he wrote in his diary.

Even more incredibly, this changed nothing. In fact, now that she had yielded to him again, it seemed entirely natural that she should claim her due from him without any ill feeling.

"There is no hope now," he wrote two days later.

He really did not hope for any improvement. Her body would lie next to him, but not the woman herself. Her mind would be elsewhere, just as before, and he would be obliged to pay her price, hour after hour. Willingly or not, he would keep his side of the bargain and listen to her talking about this absent man whom he had every reason to detest.

He hoped that when the crisis passed she would no longer feel the need to unburden herself. He could imagine what would happen next: their pact would break down, and their relationship with it.

And that is what happened. Their meetings grew less frequent and then ceased. He tried to reconcile himself to the situation. Now they were just friends.

"Are you back together again?" he asked her one day.

She nodded yes. He was sustained by the hope that she would go through another crisis which he, to his shame, could turn to his benefit.

Somewhat more relaxed, yet with the bitterness that this new situation brought him, he turned the conversation to the news reports about Albanian gangsters. There had been more of them recently. Rovena shrugged her shoulders dismissively.

Much later, on the terrace of a café, she mentioned Besfort, and the Slovak suddenly asked why he was scared of The Hague.

She had laughed. "Scared of The Hague? I don't think he is."

"I meant to say, scared of a journey to The Hague."

She shook her head. "I would say the opposite. We were going to go there together for pleasure. To visit Holland and see the tulip fields . . ."

"But The Hague isn't just a flower garden. More than anything else, it's a court. It preys on the mind of anyone with an uneasy conscience," he said.

"Oh, I see what you mean," she said, frankly showing her irritation. "But I told you, we were going there for pleasure, for the tulips."

"No, you listen to me," he said. "He saw a court summons in that dream, not tulip adverts."

They stared angrily at each other, speechless.

"What do you know about it?" she said icily.

Instead of answering, he held his head in his hands. "I'm sorry," he said amid sobs. "I'm sorry. I shouldn't have said that."

When he took his hands away, she saw that he had really been crying. "I'm disgusting," he went on in a broken voice. "I'm mad with jealousy. I don't know what I'm saying."

She waited for him to calm down and took his hand in hers, asking gently, "How do you know what he saw in his dream?"

After he had wiped away his tears, his eyes looked larger, defenceless.

"You told me yourself . . . when you wanted to show me how complicated he . . ."

She remained silent, biting her lower lip, while to herself she said, oh God.

Several years later Janek B.'s notes enabled Rovena's friend in Switzerland to recall in a new light the short phone conversation she had had with her during her northward journey. A detail that had seemed a slip of the tongue had unlocked the whole mystery of The Hague.

"Hallo, darling. Is that you? So pleased you called. Where are you calling from?"

"Can you imagine? From Denmark, from a train."

"Really?"

"I'm going to see Besfort."

"Wonderful!"

"I can see windmills, tulip fields."

"Tulip fields?"

"I mean . . . some flowers a bit like tulips . . . I don't know their names."

"Never mind. So it means you're back together again . . . Hello? I can't hear very well. Bye for now, darling."

"Bye."

What an idiot I am, Rovena thought, putting down the phone. I can't even keep a simple promise. "Don't tell anybody about this trip to The Hague," Besfort had said. Lightly, she had asked why not, and he had answered just as airily: "No reason, let's just make it a secret trip. Everybody should make a secret journey at least once in their lives." And she had cheerfully agreed.

In a second phone call, he explained that in such little subterfuges the best way not to get caught out when people ask you where you're going is to substitute another destination, for example, Denmark instead of Holland. "Let's say a trip to Denmark to see the places where the story of *Hamlet* really happened. While we're on the subject, do you have a pen? Write down Jutland, that's the province, and Saxo Grammaticus, who wrote its first history. With an 'x' and double 'm'. That's enough. No need to get mixed up with all that endless 'to be or not to be', OK?"

What an idiot, thought Rovena again. She tried to forget her blunder. She had prepared herself so carefully for this journey that it was silly to worry about something so trivial. She had a surprise ready, besides her new lingerie: two little tattoos, one between her navel and her breasts and the other on her rear. So they would be visible in whatever position they made love. She also had a stock of sweet nothings to whisper, although she couldn't be sure if she was still entitled to use them or not.

The monotonous sound of the train lulled her to sleep. You've exhausted me, she thought, thinking of Besfort waiting for her.

The words of a song, probably one she had never heard but had dreamt up in her imagination, kept coming back to her:

> If I could live my life anew
> I'd give myself again to you.

A second life, she thought. Easy to say, but so far nobody had ever been given a second life, still less the chance to go on loving someone in this other life. Yet people would never give up the hope of it, and neither would she and Besfort. They had a kind of faint, extremely faint, conception of this forbidden life. In their fear of it, the fear especially of reaching too far and thus bringing down the wrath of heaven, they were pretending they did not love each other at all.

She woke up smiling after her short sleep. As a small girl she had enjoyed this kind of self-deception, arranging facts to suit herself.

Such secrecy, she thought. Janek's imagination would run riot. Any one of Besfort's instructions would chill the blood of a woman going to meet her lover ... "Not a word to a soul about this trip. Destroy the train tickets and every shred of evidence. I'll tell you the reason later."

Words came over the loudspeaker in Dutch, then in English. They were arriving at The Hague. She phoned his mobile a third time, but still there was no reply.

She found a taxi easily, and then the hotel. A Dutch name, with no crown.

There was no message for her at reception, apart from an instruction to show her to Besfort Y.'s room. He himself was not there.

She looked round the spacious room. His two suitcases were there. His razor and his familiar aftershave were in the bathroom. On a small table was a bouquet of flowers and a card of welcome in English from the hotel manager. No message from him.

She sank into an armchair and sat there for a moment, totally drained. Saxo Grammaticus. Jutland ... He might have left some sort of sign. I will be there at such and such a time. Or simply, wait for me in the room.

Her gaze wandered involuntarily to the telephone. She stood up to call again, and one of the suitcases suddenly struck her as unfamiliar. The second one too. With a cold stab, the idea struck her that she had been given the wrong room. She rushed into the bathroom to settle her doubts, and all her sense of security evaporated. Didn't lots of men use that aftershave?

She opened the wardrobe doors. He had the habit of hanging up his shirts as soon as he checked in, but none of them were there. She looked at the two suitcases again, and automatically opened the catch of one. Before she saw any of the contents, a large envelope slipped out and fell on the bed. She was about to put it back when a bundle of photographs slid out of it. With trembling hands she bent down to collect them, and screamed. One photo showed a blood-spattered child. So did the others. What should she do? Was this the room of a serial killer? Should she shout for help, run outside to call the police?

Nobody must know that you are coming to The Hague . . . She bent down to look at the envelope again. It was addressed to "Besfort Y. Council of Europe. Crisis Department. Strasbourg."

It was for him.

Oh God. But alongside her horror there was a kind of relief. At least he really was at the Council of Europe. The address on the envelope proved this, and also that someone had sent the photos to him, perhaps as blackmail, or to remind him of something.

The ringing of the phone made her jump. She cleared her throat before lifting the receiver. It was him. She could barely grasp half of what he said. He was sorry but he would be late.

"Something has happened," she said.

"Really?"

"I can't talk about it on the phone."

"I can tell that from your voice. Why don't you take a short walk? It's a nice city. I'll be there at five o'clock."

She did what he said. Outside, her fears eased and seemed less plausible. Her feet carried her down an attractive street. All her earlier suspicions seemed crazy. Her nerves must be shattered. For the second time she thought she heard someone talking Albanian. She had heard that nervous breakdowns often started like this, with imaginary voices.

Standing in front of a shop window, she heard the voices again. She stood rooted to the spot as the voices moved away. Only then did she turn her head to look. A small group of men were moving away, talking noisily. She had never imagined that there could be so many Albanians in The Hague. Perhaps this was why Besfort so insisted on secrecy.

She entered the first café she saw. From behind the window, the street looked even prettier. She was no longer surprised at hearing Albanians talking, in loud voices as usual. They were smoking. She heard the words "today's session", the insult "arsehole" and then the name of Milošević. Everything was clear. The great courtroom building must be nearby.

She sipped her coffee without turning her head. Suddenly she recognised a familiar face. The man was sitting alone at his table, listening to the foreigners' noisy conversation with unconcealed curiosity. Surely she had seen this man before. Then she remembered. He was a distinguished writer. At any other time it would have been natural to strike up a conversation with him. She was studying in Austria, which was the writer's own country, but she remembered his pro-Serbian views and the desire to speak to him melted away.

Besfort was no doubt at the Tribunal. This explained the nightmare about the summons, the shouting in his sleep and the secrecy.

She imagined him lost in the labyrinthine corridors of the

court building. Time passed slowly. More noisy customers sat down at the table next to the Austrian, who had ordered a second coffee and seemed to be paying particular attention to what his neighbours were talking about.

Rovena preferred to think about the hotel bed. Like in the train, she felt the tattoos on her body move as if they were living creatures. In the train, the thought of the tattoo on her rear had momentarily made her head reel. She was sure he would like it, especially as they did not often make love in that position.

In a stupor of desire she ordered another tea. The photos of the children were now far from her mind. The clock hands hurried forward, as if shaken from sleep. She had a feeling she was late.

In bed in the hotel one hour later, the same feeling persisted. They had made love, without saying any of the things she had imagined.

"You told me that something had happened."

"That's right. But it's hard to talk about it."

"I understand. A lot of things are hard to talk about at first. Then . . ."

"What then?"

"There is nothing in the world that can't be talked about."

"I think there is."

"Perhaps that's because you are a woman."

"Maybe."

"What have you been doing all this time?"

"You mean since we last saw each other?" She wanted to scream: "What have I been doing? Nothing, I mean everything." But all she said was, "Why do you want to know?"

"Then don't tell me if you don't want to," he said calmly. "We put all this behind us a long time ago."

Quickly, and secretly hoping that he might understand only half of what she said, she told him how frightened she had been when, after arriving at the hotel, she thought she had been given the wrong room, because his bags had looked unfamiliar, though the aftershave was the same.

She lowered her voice and explained that, to make sure that it was really him by recognising at least one of his possessions, she had for the first time ever opened one of his suitcases.

She had the impression that he was not paying any attention. So much the better, she thought. But she did not dare say anything more.

"Shall we sleep a bit?" he said. "I've had a very tiring day. So have you, I think."

After his breathing settled into sleep, she was able to think clearly again. Mentally, she told him about what happened after she opened the bag, the macabre photographs, her terror. She calmly asked him if he was really frightened of a summons of the kind that he saw in his dreams. What connected him to these murdered children? And why had they come to The Hague secretly, skulking like criminals?

Slightly relieved, she managed to doze for a few moments. She tried to imagine how he would reply. In the worst case, his face would cloud over and his gaze become stony. Who are you to ask questions like that? You're just a call girl, a classy hooker and no more than that.

Before they went down to dinner, she sat in front of the mirror longer than usual.

He stared at her with amazement over the restaurant table. "You've become more beautiful," he said softly.

Rovena could not keep her eyes off him.

"You say that with a certain regret, I think."

"Regret? Why?"

Rovena became flustered.

"Well . . . now . . . now that we're different . . . In fact, I wanted to say . . . Do you want me ugly now . . .?"

"No, no. I would ask for anything but that."

"In fact, that's not exactly what I wanted to say . . . what I really wanted to ask was . . . In the hotel, when you fell asleep, I couldn't put these questions out of my mind . . ."

Hurriedly, as if fearful that her courage would desert her, she blurted out all of her suspicions. He looked stern, and she thought her worst fears were realised. Who are you to interrogate me like this? You're a call girl, that's all.

You've no right to call me that. Yes, you've turned me into a high-class whore, but once you were my husband.

These words went unspoken, but she caught her breath in shock.

She was frightened as always, but less of him than of the truth.

He thought carefully before replying. "Yes, those were photographs of murdered children. But not what you might have imagined. They were Serbian children, victims of the NATO bombing."

Rovena listened, nonplussed. She bit her lips and repeated twice or three times, "I'm sorry."

She had nothing to apologise for. It would be terrible to find photographs like that in any bag. She had every right to think what she liked. She could even suspect that he, Besfort, was a murderer of children. In fact, the photographs had been sent to him for that very purpose, to mark him as a murderer.

Fearfully, she clasped his hand. His fingers looked longer and thinner. He talked as if she were not there. What was happening was difficult to describe. It was a macabre photograph competition: pictures of Serbian children torn apart by bombs and of Albanian children ripped open by knives were distributed by each side to departments, commissions and committees. Grotesque slanging matches followed. Was there or was there not a scale of horror in death? Some insisted that every child's death was a tragedy that could not be compared to any other, and they could not be ranked in order. Others took a different view: the death of a child in a road accident was not the same as the death of a child in an air raid, and both were quite different from the murder of a baby, slit open by a knife wielded by a human hand. Eight hundred Albanian infants butchered like lambs, often before their mothers' eyes. It could drive you insane. It was apocalyptic.

The candles on the table danced gently in the breath of his speech. She hoped they would distract his attention.

After dinner, in the late-night bar, she mentioned her tattoos, and the tattooist's question of why she wanted them: as a memento of somebody, a promise or for some other reason.

This time, unlike on previous occasions, he did not want to hear anything more about the other man who had touched her body. He seemed to be thinking about their conversation in the restaurant.

Rovena found it difficult to talk about anything else until she had unburdened her mind. She thought about the photographs and the macabre contest, and she asked why, if he did not feel guilty, he still seemed to have something on his conscience.

He gave a chill smile.

"Because I am a citizen, meaning that everything to do with the *civitas* affects me."

Rovena did not understand what he meant, but did not say so.

As if aware of this, he went on to explain gently that quite apart from what he had said about the Albanian children he also felt grief over the Serbian children. But unfortunately that's not what happens in the Balkans. In the restaurant, she had asked why they had come here to The Hague in secret, like two criminals. She should realise that he had not been served any summons, except once or twice in his dreams. And even if he were summoned, he would not obey the court order, but only his own conscience. Every person should come to The Hague, as though it were an agency of Hades. Each for the sake of his own soul. In silence and semi-secretly.

Rovena thought of the Austrian's beard and his dull eyes, as he sat in the café among its Albanian customers.

As he spoke, Besfort looked round for the waiter, to order his second and final whisky.

It was after midnight, in bed before they made love, that he remembered the tattooist. Was he polite, handsome, a lecher? A little bit of all those things, she replied. And he made the mistake every man makes these days: as soon as he discovered that the tattoo was for a lover, he interpreted the woman's yielding as if it was to himself.

As so often, Rovena's story was left incomplete. While she was in the bathroom, he switched on the television and surfed the channels. Most were in Dutch. On one, he thought he heard Albania mentioned. He found the news in English.

"The queen has died," he said to Rovena, as she returned to the bedroom.

She lifted her eyebrows in surprise. "But that was months ago, don't you remember? We were in that motel, in Durrës."

"Of course I remember. But this is another queen. The king's wife, not his mother."

"I see, how extraordinary," she said.

On the screen, the black motorcade slowly approached the cathedral in Tirana.

Covering her bare shoulders, Besfort also expressed surprise. "How very . . . For a small country, once Stalinist, to have two queens die . . . In such a short time."

Trembling, she held him tightly.

Chapter Thirteen

The last seven days.

It was hard to tell if either of them felt any foreboding one week before the accident.

Rovena, taking shelter from the torrential rain in a café, thought about her lover's arrival. At precisely that moment, one thousand kilometres away, Besfort's thoughts, as he watched the television news, wandered to Rovena's white belly and the possibility that she might be pregnant. On the screen, Pope John Paul II looked feebler than ever, but nobody could hope for any concession from him on sexual relations between men and women. Everything would have to be the same as a thousand, four thousand, forty thousand years ago. Besfort counted the remaining days until he would see Rovena, and they seemed to him too many. In the café, Rovena dialled the code for Switzerland, but suddenly recalled that phone calls cost more at peak hours, and decided to talk to her friend later.

The rain grew heavier. Passers-by caught in the downpour ran terrified for shelter. One of them seemed continually to be changing shape as his cape was blown by the wind. After the pope, Arab terrorists appeared on the screen, threatening a kneeling European hostage. Besfort closed his eyes so as not to see the blow. Rovena unthinkingly dialled Switzerland again, but remembered the peak rate. The pedestrian with the billowing cape passed by menacingly, almost clinging to the café window. He appeared spreadeagled against it, until he detached himself and flew away as if whirled by some black tornado. Perhaps that is what Plato's androgynes would look like, she thought. Besfort had mentioned them in their last phone call. She had been amused at first.

"Awesome," she said laughing, "a man and a woman in one body. No more she-loves-me, she-loves-me-not."

"And that was why the gods envied them," Besfort said, "and out of jealousy divided them. And since that time, says Plato, the two halves have been searching for each other."

"How sad," she said. The song about the two lives with the same love flashed into her mind in a garbled form, just as she had once heard it sung by a drunk in the doorway of a bar in Tirana:

> If I could live my life anew
> I'd never give myself to you.

Rovena nervously dialled the code for Switzerland a third time. A thousand kilometres away, Besfort turned off the television in disgust. The news was all so crazy.

The storm eased slightly, only to grow wilder again, although now there were only dry gusts without rain. Rovena barely managed to reach the entrance to her block. She climbed the stairs to her apartment, closed the window and stood stock still behind the double glazing. The wind howled threateningly and then whined in lamentation, as if begging for mercy. A part of the view lay in darkness, and the rest was bathed in a sickly light in which sheets of cardboard, tar paper and garbage of all kinds were blown in every direction. You could find anything out there, she thought. Empty forms, whose essences had evaporated long ago, spun round in eddies. And she thought of her tattoos, now faded, and perhaps their two halves, his half and hers, so pitilessly divided, looking for each other.

In the evening, on the television news, among the scenes of storm devastation, there was a report on an old provincial theatre whose props had been carried away by the gales. Two particularly valuable capes for *Hamlet*, one from a production of 1759 and the other from a century later, had been lost, and the theatre promised a reward for their recovery. What a ridiculous news item, thought Besfort as he switched off the television again.

He went to bed just after midnight as usual. Towards morning, he was woken by a dream.

A kind of languid desire he had never experienced before totally sapped his strength. It included grief mixed with despair to such an impossible degree as to create a limitless, immeasurable sweetness.

It was the kind of dream that lingers in the mind. There was a plateau bathed in pale light from an unknown source. In the middle was a structure of plaster and marble, a kind of mausoleum that was also a motel, towards which he was calmly walking.

He was seeing it for the first time, although the structure was not unfamiliar to him. He stood in front of what were not so much its door and windows as the places where they had once been, now covered with oily paint resembling plaster, and barely visible.

He felt that he knew why he was there. He even knew what was locked inside, because he called a name out loud. It was a woman's name, which, although he uttered it himself, he could not hear or even identify. It emerged falteringly, despairingly from his throat. He was aware merely that the name had three or four syllables. Something like Ix-et-in-a . . .

He remembered the strange continuation of the dream, and his weakness and longing became unendurable.

He turned on the bedside lamp and looked at his watch. It was half past four. It occurred to him that even dreams that seem unforgettable can later fade away.

First thing in the morning he would phone Rovena and tell her about this. He must.

This thought reassured him, and he fell asleep at once.

Part Three

I

With these two storm-battered capes, the life stories of Besfort
Y. and Rovena St. were strangely cut short a week before they
actually ended. In an explanatory note, the researcher had
repeated his position that, being unable to reproduce the
couple's story in full on the basis of the results of the inquiry,
he had concentrated on the last forty weeks of their lives. The
ending of the story with the two *Hamlet* costumes carried
away by the gale was accidental, and therefore probably could
not be taken as a symbolic closure. Still less could Besfort Y.'s
pre-dawn dream, which he related to Rovena on the phone a
few hours later, be considered in the same light. But there
may have been another reason why, in spite of all promises,
the final week – usually the most keenly anticipated in a story
of this kind – was omitted.

The more closely the researcher examined this last week,
which was at first sight so straightforward, the more signifi-
cant it became. But he was always thrown back on the problem

of its incompleteness. The three last days had detached themselves entirely from the chain of events which death had
brought to an end. These were the three days for which Besfort
Y. had requested leave from his office at the Council of Europe.
Apart from his application for leave, made orally in his final
telephone call, there was no tangible evidence of these last
three days anywhere. The testimony of the bartenders and
receptionists was vaguer than ever. There was no record of
any phone calls from their hotel room and both their mobiles
were switched off. It was as if these three days were not their
own, but were unclaimed stretches of time of the kind that
may wander around the universe unattached to any human
life, trying to find some temporary lodging. So they floated
adrift, bound to nobody, and not understood by anyone, least
of all by those in whose lives they took refuge.

In another note, the researcher strove to explain what he
called the strange "crabwise" progress of the days and weeks.
Mourning customs everywhere mark seven days and forty days
after a death, but here were periods of seven and forty
days calculated before their deaths. These in his view were
intended to convey an impression of the reverse order of time
experienced by the two lovers, if that is what they could be
called.

As he approached the zero hour, which in this looking-glass
world could have been the end, the beginning or both, or
neither of these, the researcher probably felt a rising panic.
Finally, confronted with a knot he could not unravel, he stood
to one side at the most unexpected moment.

It was obvious from the file containing the relevant evidence that this dereliction of duty when faced with the final week caused the researcher great pain. Here, totally jumbled and impossibly crammed together, were fragmentary statements and testimonies, documents, protocols; a twice-repeated request for an autopsy of Rovena's body rejected out of hand by her parents; an application for Besfort's exhumation in Tirana, which had been granted; an allegation made by Liza Blumberg that Rovena was murdered not by intelligence agencies but by Besfort Y. on the night before 17 May; a photocopy of the weather report for the fateful morning from the newspaper *Kurier*, which was relevant to this allegation; and finally the permission for three days' leave, issued in response to Besfort's last request in this life.

The researcher kept coming back to this document in the hope that it might yield more information. He could not forget what a colleague had said a long time ago, when he had first mentioned the inquiry to him. In such cases of law, the English refer to remote history, Muslims to the *Qur'an* and emergent African states to the *Encyclopedia Britannica*, but in the Balkans they find every precedent with little effort in their ballads. Three days' leave to carry out a duty, normally something left undone? There will certainly be a well-known paradigm for this.

It was in fact a cliché. Half the ballads of the Balkans included such requests. Every character seemed eager to negotiate an extended deadline. Some bargained with death; others at a later date in history, and thus on a less epic scale, asked for leave from prison. And so on until the present day, when Besfort Y. had asked for leave from his office at the Council of Europe. The cases were very different, but in essence they all shared something in common: a secret contract, from which there was no escape.

The researcher was dumbfounded. According to the experts, Besfort had asked for three days' leave from the Crisis Department in Brussels, just like Ago Ymeri had done from a medieval prison.

The researcher imagined Ago Ymeri on horseback, galloping to the church where his betrothed was about to marry another man . . . He had never heard such an inconsistent story: why had he been given leave, and why, after its expiry, was he bound to return to prison? The meaning must be encoded.

The researcher felt a sickening pang in the pit of his stomach. What help were all these shadows and shapes that so resembled each other? He thought about the taxi driver and his rear-view mirror, in which the mystery had surely been revealed, if only for an instant of time.

Latterly his researches had focused entirely on this question. "What did you see in this mirror? What was that fatal shock? Have you ever lost someone you can't ever forget? Who is so lost to you that they won't come back, even in your dreams?"

So began one of their many conversations, all so similar to each other.

"Who won't come back, even in my dreams? I don't know what to say," the man replied.

"You have a daughter of about the same age as that unknown young woman who got into your taxi. Have you ever had problems with her? For any private reason of the sort you would never reveal to a soul? That will go with you to the grave? I think you will have heard this expression, but probably without thinking hard about it. Imagine what it means to be in the grave, in this narrow chamber not just for a few days or weeks or years but for centuries, millennia, hundreds and thousands of millennia. Just you two, you and the grave. The grave and you. Narrator and audience. The stories we tell on earth are mere fragments, crumbs of the great narrative of the dead. For thousands of years, in hundreds of languages, the dead have been weaving their story. But it will remain in the grave for ever and ever. For all eternity, never heard by a living soul. Your final confidence, between you and the grave. Between the grave and you. Think of yourself there, with no advocate, no witness, afraid of nothing, because you yourself are nothing. Think of yourself like that and give me the tiniest hint, a smidgen of what you will tell to the grave. This is what I am asking you to do as a human being, a taxi driver. Do me this honour. Think of me for a moment as your brother. As your grave."

"I don't understand you. I'm tired. I'm so tired. I don't know what you want."

"Have you ever thought of impossible things? Taboos, we call them in this world. Who knows what they call them in the next. It's a tough question, but I won't apologise. The grave does not apologise."

"I'm tired. Leave me in peace. The doctor says these long sessions aren't good for me."

"You're right. Calm down. Let me ask you just two simple questions about the last moments before the accident. How did her face look? And his?"

"They were both cold. Or that's how they looked to me. Like wax, as one might say."

"Was it this that scared you, I mean confused you?"

"Perhaps."

"What else? What else happened?"

"Nothing. It went silent, like in church. Except that from outside there was a sort of dazzling light. I think that's why I couldn't see the road. The taxi seemed propelled through the air."

"You said that at that moment they were trying to kiss. I'm sorry for asking the same question as everybody else. Did this really startle you? Even scare you?"

"It seemed . . . but they seemed scared themselves. At least I saw that in the woman's eyes. In the mirror, I saw fear."

"You saw their fear in the mirror . . . But your own fear, where did you see that?"

"I don't understand you."

"Your own fear," I said. "The fear that your thought was theirs, wasn't it really your own? Have you yourself ever wanted to break a taboo of that kind? And did they remind you of this. Is that why you lost control and crashed?"

"I don't understand. Stop tiring me."

"Calm down . . . and then? What happened next? Did they manage to kiss?"

"I'm not sure. I don't think so. That was the moment of impact. Everything was smashed to pieces in the gully. The light was blinding. Devastating."

2

Each time the researcher left the taxi driver, he had a feeling that something had been left unsaid. He could hardly wait to return, to try again. Next time, he thought, he would make no mistake. The driver held the answer. He would have to give up all his philosophical speculations about two sorts of love, the old one, dating back millions of years, which operated within the tribe, and the new rebellious one that had broken out of that prison. Let others deal with the rivalry or alliance between these two sorts of love and the hopes each of them nourished of treacherously supplanting the other, when the time came. This was a mystery involving the old devices of the world, which from one millennium to the next, in semi-darkness, had shaped the savagery of tigers and the soul's lusts, pity, shame or hours of peace. He had nothing to do with these things, or with ballads, ancient or modern. His business was with the driver, who perhaps imagined that he had got off scot-free and was out of his clutches. And he had every right to think this as long as the researcher had still not put the fatal question: was he an accessory to murder or not?

That question will come. It will come, my precious. As soon as he had settled various side issues. Then he could forget all those ballads. Or so he imagined, until a moment came when he was compelled to ask himself why he was so fixated on them.

He could easily imagine the horseman with his bride behind him, and the conversation between the two.

"Where are we going? To . . . the prison?"

"Of course to the prison, where else?"

"But what will I do there? And does the law allow this?"

"I never thought of that."

"But why? What did you agree to? Why did they let you go? What did you promise them?"

Drumming hooves filled the silence. Then words again.

"Why do you have to go back? Let's run away, both of us. We are free."

"I can't."

"Why not? What's holding you back?"

Silence again, and the hooves raising dust.

"Can't we rest a bit?"

"No, we're late. This is my third day of leave. The prison gate closes at nightfall."

"What is that river there? It looks like the one where we first met by the bridge, remember? Why has it turned against us?"

"We have to hurry. Hold on to me tight."

"But what are those sheep? Those black oxen? Why all this traffic?"

"We've got to hurry. Hold tight."

"Ago, what are you doing? You're strangling me . . ."

"Perhaps we'll arrive before the gate closes. Airports are strict nowadays. Boarding gates are closing earlier all the time."

With half-closed eyes the researcher shook his head. He could not believe this. A hunch told him that, before his next meeting with the driver, he should visit Lulu Blumb.

Unlike the first time, at these later meetings with the researcher, Lulu Blumb was extremely careful to advance the suspicion that Besfort Y. was a murderer only at a late stage in the interview and after the utmost deliberation.

This was evidently why Lulu Blumb, before coming to the essential point of her story, which later featured most prominently in the conclusion to the inquiry, carefully explained various profound and subtle issues of the kind that she was better placed to know than anyone else. For instance, apologising to the researcher for putting it bluntly, she said with a good deal of pride that many men may have slept with Rovena, but none of them could claim to know the intimate parts of her body better than she did. The researcher expected a comparison with the piano, which she indeed mentioned in passing, before dwelling on the idea that her fingers had transposed the music of Mozart and Ravel, against whose background they had met and later made love, from the keyboard of the nightclub piano to her body. With a sardonic smile, she added that she did not believe that the tedious and often barbarous statements of the Council of Europe about military intervention, terrorism, bombing and other horrors, which were Besfort's stock in trade, went very well with lovemaking.

Always along the same lines, and evidently wishing to postpone as long as possible the moment when she pointed the finger of blame, Liza Blumberg dispelled some of the mystery surrounding an aspect of the crime that had baffled many. She was as much tortured by pangs of conscience at not having rescued Rovena from Besfort as by grief at her death.

She kept saying this was the first time she had ever been defeated by a man.

During endless days and nights, Lulu Blumb vainly racked her brains. How had Besfort kept the woman he loved so enchained? How had he so terrorised her? How had he made her so sick?

Usually men behaved like complete fools when they discovered that their rival was a woman. They sniggered or felt relieved that it was not another man that had ousted them. Some were devoured by curiosity, and others hoped to beguile their rival. Later, when they knew the truth, they would beat their heads with their fists and curse the day they had grinned like apes instead of howling in dismay.

Lulu Blumb had waited impatiently for that moment. She waited until it dawned on her that it would never come. Besfort would never grow jealous of her. She would be jealous of him. This was the difference between them, which handed the victory to him instead of to her.

The two rivals knew about each other, but in different ways. When Rovena once mentioned a new experience with Besfort, the pianist had cut her off, saying she did not want to know. Rovena retorted that Besfort was quite the opposite and wanted to know everything. At this moment Lulu Blumb went pale.

"What do you mean, the opposite?"

It was too late for Rovena to put together a soothing reply . . . The opposite meant that not only did he not stand in the way of her seeing Lulu, but he even liked to hear . . . meaning he enjoyed . . . and he even encouraged her, whenever she quarrelled with Lulu, to make up.

"You slut," Liza shouted. Rovena, she said, had used their love to excite that bastard's lust. She had marketed it like some porno film. Like an idiot, she had allowed herself to be used like a doll. Do you understand what I mean? Do you understand German? Do you know what "doll" means? A dummy! That's how he used you. Like those pimps from your country who put their fiancées on the street. You've read the newspapers and heard the radio. But you didn't stop there. You dragged me into this game. And his lordship, this generous scumbag, gives his permission for you to come to me. In other words, he throws me charity in the shape of yourself. Because that's what you've been reduced to, a dummy. And that's what I've become, a beggar at the church door.

Rovena listened in bewilderment to Liza's sobbing, which was so much harder to endure than her rage. Besfort wasn't jealous, because she counted for nothing. To his Balkan male mentality, she, Lulu Blumb, was an object of ridicule, a plaything, a soap bubble, a distraction for Rovena while she remained enslaved to him. She apologised for the word "slut", and all the other things. She admitted that she could not compete with that monster. She accepted defeat. Perhaps it would be better if they did not meet any more. She had nothing more to say except: God help you!

Rovena wept too. She also begged forgiveness. She told Lulu that she shouldn't take all these things so much to heart. In the end, he was her husband.

"Husband?" she wailed through her sobs. This was the first she had heard of it . . . In fact, it was true . . . They were keeping it secret . . . At least it was true for Rovena . . . "But you were ready to come with me to that little Greek church in the middle of the Ionian Sea to be married . . ."

"That's true, but it didn't really change anything . . . He was my husband in another sense, I mean, in another dimension . . ."

3

A secret husband, another dimension. Lulu Blumb said that he alone gave Rovena these ideas. She was totally defenceless against his malign influence. Of course it wasn't easy. To her horror, even Lulu found herself affected. Her hatred for him gave her no protection.

Her proposal of marriage was the first occasion on which she felt she had successfully challenged him. Rovena's misery as she walked with Besfort among the churches of Vienna, without entering any of them to be married, gave Lulu the idea that these churches were not theirs and that she herself could take her to a different shrine dedicated to another kind of love.

Was there really some remote chapel somewhere between Greece and Albania where lesbians married, or was all this mere fantasy?

There had been rumours of such a place for a long time, but nobody could pin down the location. There were no pointers to any travel agency or marriage bureau, not a trace on the internet. Of course there were suspicions that trafficking was involved. There was talk of a secret network that procured young women and offered a wedding for three thousand euros, plus three days of bliss with the partner of your heart's desire, in a fabulous little hotel. The rest was easy to imagine. Greek and Albanian boat owners, who once ferried clandestine migrants, now disembarked these protesting women on deserted coasts, pretending they had lost their way in the storm. There they raped them, put them back on the boat, carried them round in circles and abandoned them again on some remote beach, or worse, drowned them. Or, driven by some incomprehensible fury, the boat owners threw themselves into the sea and perished with the shrieking women.

Rovena knew nothing about this. Lulu Blumb, though terrified by the rumours, still could not give up the idea of this journey.

Sometimes this project seemed to her nothing less than a temptation generated by the vicious imagination of her rival. Besfort Y. was also probably in search of an alternative church for Rovena and himself. A different sort of church, for their extraordinary relationship.

Perhaps he was frightened by the reality of this world and felt estranged from it. This could be why he was in search of another dimension. And, as usual, he had managed to infect Rovena with the same obsession.

A short time before her death, one morning before dawn, Rovena had woken in tears and related to Lulu a dream that she had just had: she had been asking for a ticket at an airport desk, but there had been no room on the plane. She had pleaded and entreated. She needed to go home to Albania, where two queens had died one after another – she was the third one, but she was still abroad. The member of staff had said, "Madam, you're on the waiting list as an ordinary passenger, not as a queen." But Rovena insisted that she was a genuine queen. She was expected at the cathedral in Tirana and she had two changes of clothes, because she did not know why she was going there, for her wedding or for her funeral . . .

Evidently, like so many young women in this world, she was sometimes a slave and sometimes a queen, and could not find her natural place.

The pianist was unable to give clear answers to the researcher's many questions about the new kind of love that the couple were apparently looking for.

At least that is how she understood it until one day she began to suspect something else. It occurred to Lulu Blumb that these two, in their quest for a still unimagined form of love, were like voluntary patients who agree to test the effects of new and dangerous medicines.

As she had once explained, Besfort, like every difficult personality, felt isolated in the world. Perhaps his quest for a new form of love was connected to this. It was a love that excluded infidelity, yet he also understood that no passionate relationship between a woman and a man can be cemented without the risk of loss. This was evidently the reason why he had willingly exposed their love to this danger, and had divided it into two phases: the first, secure in the past, as if sealed in a bottle, and the second, in which Rovena was no longer his beloved, but simply a call girl.

The researcher himself had told her that they had used the expression *post mortem* for this second phase. Both had used the phrase, but in fact she was *post mortem* while he was not. With the introduction of this phrase, she began to die. The project of her murder was contained in essence, if unconsciously, inside it.

It was natural that Besfort should come to this idea. Tyrannical natures prefer radical solutions. He had used every means to accustom himself to the idea of her infidelity. When he saw that none of them preserved him from the anguish of loss, he decided to do what thousands of people in this world do: get rid of his beloved.

Lulu Blumb had detected his inclination to murder before the intelligence agencies started talking about it. His terror of a summons by The Hague Tribunal, the photos of the murdered children in his bag, and Rovena's tattoos, which were only reflections of his own desires – all these things were sure indications. His passion for destruction was obvious whenever anything stood in his way: an idea, a state, such as Yugoslavia, a cause, a religion, a woman and maybe even his own people.

Rovena had come up against him when she was only twenty-three, and he could not fail to kill her.

They racked their brains to understand why he had virtually turned her into a prostitute. They thought they had found the reason, and pretended as much, but they hadn't. Gangsters and pimps who whored out their fiancées for dollars were easier to understand than Besfort. Lulu herself had produced some very complicated rationalisations. What if it was very simple, and turning her into a call girl was merely a prelude to murder? After all, in this world, when women are killed, prostitution is the first thing you think of.

She did not want to expand it any further. She was not going to analyse the famous dream with the plaster mausoleum, which was quite obviously a typical murderer's dream.

If the researcher, for his own or professional reasons, was averse to psychological subtleties, he could forget everything she had said so far and listen only to one thing, the basic explanation which she had given long ago, that Besfort Y. murdered his girlfriend because she had found out his secret depths . . .

4

The pianist drew a deep breath. She knew that moment at concerts when, after a long silence, the listeners simultaneously breathe again.

These secrets were spine-chilling, she continued. They involved NATO, and internal rifts that could have divided the entire West. If the investigators were scared, what about herself, a defenceless musician?

She talked about this fear, but her interrogator interrupted her gently. Miss Blumb, he said, you have mentioned two quite distinct motives for murder. You called the first psychotic, and this one might be considered political. May I ask you, which one do you believe yourself?

The pianist carefully considered her reply: she believed both of them, but the psychotic motive was probably decisive. The second was a pretext found by Besfort to justify the murder to himself.

Liza lowered her voice, but he kept listening. He had to steer his mind away from the trap into which all the other investigators had fallen. If Rovena St. was no longer alive on the morning of 17 May, another woman must have been beside Besfort in the taxi going to the airport.

You said that the murder took place earlier, he whispered. But what about the body? Why wasn't it found?

According to her, it was up to the police to find the body. They themselves were talking about a quite different matter. It was vital that he should believe her. She pleaded with him. He must believe that she had been murdered. She almost fell to her knees. Don't insult her memory by refusing to believe this . . . She had been murdered, for sure, but she could not say exactly where . . .

He could barely follow her. Finally, he grasped the thread of her argument, but it was so thin and frail. If he did not believe in the murder, it meant he did not believe in their love. Because, as they now knew, their love and the murder were testimonies to each other, and if there was proof of their love there were no grounds to doubt the murder.

The interrogator's incredulous smile was enough to make Lulu Blumb lose her way.

Breaking a final silence, the longest of all, she admitted that it was natural for a researcher like himself to misinterpret her insistence that Rovena St. and Besfort Y. had not been together on that fatal taxi ride on the morning of 17 May. He might see it as a final attempt on the part of the pianist, who had tried to separate them in life, to divide them in death. He had every right to think this way, but she would be honest with him to the end. To convince him that there had been a murder, she would tell him her greatest secret, something that she had never confessed to anybody and had been sure she would carry with her to the grave. She too, Liza Blumberg, had plotted to murder Rovena . . .

Her terrible plan involved the remote chapel by the Ionian Sea. She knew of the atrocities that took place there, the women thrown into the sea while the insane boatmen howled with laughter. But she had not been afraid. Until the very end, she had dreamed of a journey from which neither she nor Rovena would ever return. If the boatmen did not throw her into the sea, she herself would have thrown her arms around her lover's neck and dragged her down into the deep . . . But apparently what should have happened at sea was fated to happen on land, in a taxi. As always, Lulu Blumb was too late. After this confession, she was sure that her interrogator would understand that her anger at Besfort Y., like any anger against a fellow murderer, could only be of the feeblest sort. She hoped that when the time came for her soul to seek rest, she would pray for him with the same tenderness as for herself.

5

The researcher was sure that Lulu Blumb would never talk to him again after her shocking confession. There had been something conclusive about her story, like the closing of a door, that dashed any hopes of a sequel.

The researcher was stabbed by remorse at not having delved deeper into certain dark episodes in her story. He had noticed that whenever Lulu Blumb said that she would not elaborate on certain aspects of her tale, it was precisely these points that were most important, and to which his mind kept reverting.

For instance, he had not properly asked about the second dream. He kicked himself for this, and in self-punishment he mentally replayed this dream again and again, just as he had heard it from the Albanian woman in Switzerland.

She had described Besfort Y. walking across the wasteland towards the funereal building. He stands in front of the mausoleum that is also a motel, with doors that are at the same time not doors. He knows why he is there, and he also doesn't know. A cold light emanates from the plaster and the marble. He calls out the name of a woman, but without even hearing what name his lips utter. This woman is evidently within the marble, because he calls to her again, but his voice emerges so feebly that he can hardly hear it. A gleam of light that he had not noticed until then comes from inside and he knocks on the painted glass. He hears a slight sound as a door opens, where he thought there was none. The night porter of the motel, or the temple guard, appears. "There's no such woman here," he says, and closes the door again.

Meanwhile, a woman indeed appears, descending the winding external stairway which leads perhaps from a terrace. Her tight skirt makes her appear taller. Her face is unfamiliar. Stepping off the final stair, she comes up to him and throws her arm round his neck. He feels an infinite tenderness and sweetness, but he cannot catch her name, which she utters in the faintest of voices. She says something else. Perhaps it is about her long wait inside, or how much she has missed him. But he cannot understand anything of what she says. He realises only that something is missing.

The woman lowers her head to tell him her name, or just to kiss him, but still something is missing and he wakes up.

Over time, this dream expanded in his mind, as if leavened by memory.

It was easy to interpret this as a murderer's dream. The dreamer comes to a place in which he has been happy, and so the building resembles a motel. But it also resembles a tomb, which shows that at the place where he was happy, he has also killed.

Lulu Blumb insisted on this explanation. The researcher did not dare contradict her, but still looked for another one. Besfort Y. goes to that tract of wasteland looking for whoever is inside the building, frozen or immured. He calls out, summoning her, to thaw her. But it is not easy for her either.

But that's almost the same, Lulu Blumb would say. There's no doubt that it is Rovena inside, under all that plaster or marble. Buried, in every sense of the word.

The researcher continued his imaginary dialogue with Lulu Blumb, with a premonition that they would meet again.

Which they did. Her phone call gave him a boyish thrill.

They tried to postpone the subject as long as they could, but the conversation soon came round to their common obsession. Clearly Lulu too had been mentally rehearsing her questions, answers and objections. Try as they might to keep their heads clear, the moment came when each of them confused the other, although they knew very well that they shouldn't allow themselves to be ensnared by the dream of a third person, reported by a fourth, if not a fifth.

Lulu was the first to dispel the mist. She returned doggedly to the morning of 17 May, when the taxi waited in the rain in front of the hotel. The temperature was 7° Celsius, the wind variable and the rain incessant.

The researcher listened hard, but could not forget the dream. What was Besfort looking for behind that marble, inside that desolate building, after midnight? Rovena, of course, but which one? Rovena murdered, spoiled? And why did she not come out to him where he expected, but by way of the winding stairway? Repentance was there, of course. But who repented? Besfort? Rovena? Both? And for what? He wanted to ask Lulu Blumb, but she was a long way away.

6

Her voice was very determined. To her credit, she had been the only person not to rest content with the explanations given for the very long interval between the couple's departure from the hotel and the moment of the accident. She had collected astonishingly precise evidence relating to the morning of 17 May, newspaper articles, weather bulletins and the traffic reports provided by the police for the radio. This precision struck everybody as at least giving her the right to a hearing. Her evidence also recreated with appalling vividness the atmosphere in the lobby of the Miramax Hotel that morning: the chandeliers, whose light grew pale as day dawned, the sleepy night porter, Besfort Y. going to the desk to settle his bill and order a taxi, then returning to the lift, going up to the room and coming back with his girlfriend, whom he held tight as he led her from the door of the lift to the waiting cab. The porter, interrogated dozens of times, always said the same thing: after a sleepless night, twenty minutes before the end of his shift, neither he nor anybody else would be able to clearly recognise a woman, most of whose face was hidden by the raised collar of her rain-coat, by her hat and the shoulder of the man to whom she seemed almost bound. Still less could the waiting driver see anything but two vague silhouettes approaching his car through the pelting rain and the wind that changed direction at every moment.

Liza Blumberg insisted that the young woman who entered the taxi was not . . . the normal Rovena. Asked what she meant by this, she replied that the young woman, even if she were Rovena, could only have been her shape, her replica.

At this point she produced the photos taken immediately after the accident, none of which showed the woman's face. Besfort's face was clearly visible, with his eyes immobile and a trickle of blood, as if drawn by a pen, on his right temple. But of the young woman who had fallen on her stomach alongside him, only her chestnut hair and her right arm stretched across his body were visible.

The pianist had repeated this story several times to earlier interviewers. To Lulu's annoyance, they had listened with more sympathy than attention. Her anger forced them to enter into a discussion with her, but they proceeded without enthusiasm. Let us concede the possibility that the murder took place earlier. How would she then explain Besfort's behaviour afterwards? Why would he drag a stiffened corpse, or a replica, into a taxi? Where would he take it and how would he get rid of it, with or without the driver's help?

This took Lulu aback, but only for a moment. Of course the

driver might have been involved. But this was a secondary matter. The important thing was to find out what happened to Rovena. Liza Blumberg believed that Rovena was murdered away from the hotel, and that Besfort Y., whether with assistance or not, had disposed of the body. But he needed that body, or something in the shape of Rovena, at the moment of leaving the hotel. They had stayed there two nights, so when the time came to search for the vanished woman, the first person to ask would be her lover or partner, call him what you like. His reply was easy to imagine: he and his girlfriend had both left the hotel early in the morning. She had accompanied him to the airport as usual, and had then disappeared on the way back. Everything would be simple and convincing, except that he needed something: a body, a shape.

Under her interviewers' increasingly despondent gaze, Lulu Blumb elaborated her theory. Besfort Y. needed a shape or simulacrum of Rovena, the woman whom he had destroyed, body and soul.

He must have brooded for a long time over his alibi. And who or what would be a suitable substitute for the dead woman? What at first seemed frightening or impossible was simpler on close examination. He could easily find a more or less similar woman, at least of the same height, and bring her to the hotel. Or, if not a woman, something mute, without memory, and so without danger, such as a dummy, of the kind sold in every sex shop. Before dawn, in the gloom of the hotel lobby, it would be hard for a drowsy porter to notice that the woman emerging from the lift, in the close embrace of her lover, was different . . .

239

The interviewers grew weary and began to show their impatience. This happened with the first interviewer, the second and the fourth. Liza came to expect this, and so at her first meeting with the researcher, when the time came to talk about this day (the morning with its rain and wind that gave the hotel lobby an even more desolate air as Besfort Y. carried the simulacrum of his girlfriend to the taxi), she gave a guilty smile and spoke quickly, trying in vain to avoid uttering the word "dummy" and mumbling it under her breath.

This word changed everything. The researcher was visibly shaken.

"You mentioned an imitation, a dummy, if I am not mistaken."

The guilty smile on Lulu's face froze into a grin. "If you don't like the word, forget it. I meant something in Rovena's place, something artificial, sort of contrived."

"Miss Blumberg, there is no reason why you should dodge the issue. Did you say the word 'dummy' or not. The word you used was *ein Mannequin*."

Liza Blumb wanted to apologise for her German, but the researcher had grabbed hold of her hand. She was scared. She expected to hear insults from him, of the kind the others had thought but left unsaid. Instead, to her amazement, without releasing her hand, he said softly, "My dear lady."

It was her turn to wonder if he had really said these words, or if her ears were deceiving her.

His eyes looked hollow, as if their gaze were turned back into his skull.

7

In fact, the researcher's mind was thrown into total disarray. Here was the solution to the riddle he had been pursuing for so long. He wanted to say: "Miss Blumberg, you have given me the key to the mystery," but he lacked the energy to speak.

The secret appeared suddenly out of the surrounding mist. What the driver had seen in the rear-view mirror had been nothing but an imitation. His human passenger had tried to kiss a replica. Or the replica, the person.

This was the crux. The other questions – where Rovena had been killed, if there had really been a murder, and why (the NATO secrets, the most likely motive), where they had dumped her or her body and what was done later with the dummy – these were all secondary considerations.

"Oh God," he said aloud. Now he remembered that somewhere in his inquiry there really had been mention of a doll. A female doll torn apart by dogs.

That was where the explanation lay, nowhere else. This was

the secret that had baffled them all. And those disconcerting words, as if coming from a universe made of plastic: *Sie versuchten gerade, sich zu küssen*. They were trying to kiss.

A doll had been behind everything, a soulless object that would serve to get Besfort out of the hotel. Then the story would continue on the autobahn to the airport. "Stop at this service area so I can throw this thing away." Or: "Take these euros and get rid of it for me."

Neither of these things happened, because of the kiss. It was this incident that startled the driver and brought the story to an abrupt close. Instead of throwing out the doll, they had all of them overturned.

He banged his fists on his temples. But what about the police? The first transcript had mentioned this very thing, the dummy, found alongside Besfort Y.'s body.

The researcher was in no hurry to call himself an idiot. The truth was still incomplete, but in essence he had found it. Of course, some details did not fit. There were discrepancies: the living bodies and the plastic did not match. There were differences of interpretation, and confusions of past and future. But these were temporary. It was like a group portrait: a pair of lovers, a doll, an impossible kiss and a murder. These ingredients would not assemble themselves into one picture. This was understandable: such mismatches between the conception of a murder and its enactment were familiar. Sometimes a murder and its victim would not come together, as if they had confused their schedules, until eventually they found each other.

The researcher strove to reduce what had happened to its

simplest elements, as if it were an after-dinner story. Shortly after the taxi had left the hotel, the driver noticed that his passenger, muffled in her overcoat and scarf, seemed more like a doll than a living woman. After his initial surprise, mixed with a kind of superstitious fear, he pulled himself together. Weren't there plenty of crazy people who travelled with broken violoncellos, brandy stills or tortoises, all painstakingly wrapped? So he was not unnerved at all, and even remained calm when the plastic creature appeared to show signs of life. This was an illusion, produced by the bends in the road, or because he was tired. Only when his passenger tried to kiss the doll did the taxi driver snap.

The researcher imagined different scenarios, as he was accustomed to doing for every crime. In the first, the driver was paid in advance to throw a doll into the road. In the next, more serious scenario, it was not a doll but a corpse that was to be thrown out, of course for a larger sum of money. In both versions, the strange passenger tried to kiss the figure beside him, a doll or a corpse, and that was when disaster struck.

The final and gravest version involved the taxi driver's complicity in the murder. On the way to the airport, he and Besfort were to turn off into a waste clearing, to bury the body. It was Besfort's attempt at a farewell kiss that caused the catastrophe.

8

It was early Sunday morning when, to the sound of Easter bells, he set off sleepily for the taxi driver's apartment. The city was ashen after winter. There's no hope, he thought, without being able to say of what.

The woman who opened the door glowered at him, but the taxi driver said he had been expecting him. He was now much readier to talk than before.

Everybody wants to unburden themselves, the researcher said to himself. But they passed all their burdens to him.

"I will only ask you one thing," he said in a low voice. "Please be even more precise than before."

The driver sighed. He listened to the researcher, his eyes steady. Then he hung his head for a long time. "Was it a living woman or a doll?"

He repeated what the researcher said in a low voice, as if talking to himself. "Your questions get more difficult all the time."

The researcher looked at him gratefully. He had not shouted, what's all this crazy stuff, what the hell are you driving at? He had simply said that the question was a difficult one.

Slowly, as before, he described that grim morning with its incessant sleet, the taxi engine running as he waited for his two customers. Finally they emerged from the hotel door. Clutching one another, with coat collars upturned, they hurried to the taxi. Without waiting for the driver to get out, the man opened the car's left-hand door for his girlfriend, and went round to the other side to sit down in the opposite corner, from where he ordered *Flughafen!* in a foreign accent.

As the driver had said so often, the traffic had never been so congested as that day. It crawled forward through the semi-darkness of dawn, stopped, started, came to a complete stand-still. There were refrigerated trucks, lorries, buses, all drenched in the rain, with the names of firms, shipping agencies, mobile phone numbers, reappearing to the left or right as they filtered through, as if in some nightmare. During his time in the hospital, those inscriptions in strange and frightening languages had haunted him. Words in French, Spanish, Dutch. Half of united Europe and all the Tower of Babel was there.

The researcher's eyes lost their earlier despondency. You can't spin the story out indefinitely, he thought. Whether you want to or not, at some stage you will have to answer my question.

He waited as long as he could before repeating it. The driver took a moment of silence to think.

"Yes, that business of the dummy. Whether that woman resem-bled a doll or not . . . Of course she did. Especially now that you remind me. Sometimes she looked like a dummy, and sometimes he did. As everybody does. Behind car windows with condensation, that's how most people look, distant, remote, made of wax."

The researcher felt his temper rise.

"I asked you not to dodge the question," he suddenly cried, "at least not this one. I begged you, I pleaded on my knees."

Oh God, he's started again, thought the man.

The researcher's voice was hoarse. He almost gasped.

"I gave you a last chance to tell the truth, to get all that fear gnawing you inside out of your system. Tell me, what was that thing that terrified you so much? A man trying to kiss a dummy? Or a doll trying to kiss a man? Or was something missing that made such a thing impossible for either of them? Tell me!"

"I don't know what to say. I'm not in a position to say. I can't."

"Tell me your secret."

"I can't. I don't know."

"You don't want to because you're under suspicion too. Tell me. How were you going to dispose of the body, after the murder? Where were you going to throw the dummy? Don't try and wriggle out of it! You know everything. You were keeping track of everything. In your mirror. Like a sniffer dog."

The researcher's voice subsided again. He had been so excited when he arrived at the apartment, hoping to please the driver too with his discovery. But he hadn't wanted to know. Mentally, he addressed the doll itself. Nobody wants you, he said to it. Nobody can even see you but me.

Silently he drew from his briefcase the photos of the two

victims. Would the gentleman take another look. Notice that the dead woman's face is not visible anywhere.

The man averted his eyes. He stammered in terror. Why were they pressing only him for this secret? If this victim wasn't a woman but a doll, why hadn't the police said anything?

Psychic, the researcher said to himself. This was the same first question that he had put to Liza Blumberg, after which his mind had strangely clouded over. He hadn't heard her reply.

The driver spoke haltingly. Something inexplicable had happened in his taxi. Something impossible . . . but why were they asking only him to explain?

The researcher interrupted. "You're the last person who should complain. I've asked you a thousand times why you crashed the taxi after seeing a kiss and you won't give me an answer."

They both sat in silence, stupefied with exhaustion. You might just as well ask me why I believed Liza Blumb's story, and I wouldn't know how to reply, the researcher reflected. We could all ask questions of each other. What right have we got in this pitch-black night to ask about things that are beyond our powers to see?

He was too tired to relate how years ago, at high school, he had been taken to an exhibition of modern art. The students had laughed at pictures of people with three eyes or displaced breasts, or giraffes in the form of bookcases, in flames. Don't laugh, somebody had told them. One day you'll understand that the world is more complicated than it appears.

The researcher calmed down again, and his eyes even recovered their earlier tenderness.

"There are other truths, besides those which we think we see," he said softly. "We don't know, don't want to, or can't know, or perhaps mustn't . . ." His unfortunate friend was saying that something impossible had happened in his taxi. This was perhaps the essence. Nobody knows the rest. "What happened in your taxi was something different from what you saw. They had been together on the back seat, innocent and guilty, a man and perhaps a woman who had been murdered, dolls, replicas, shapes and spirits, sometimes together and sometimes apart, like those flaming giraffes. What you saw and what I imagined are evidently very far from the truth. It was not for nothing that the ancients suspected the gods of denying us human beings their superior knowledge and wisdom. That is why our human eyes were blind, as usual, to what happened."

The investigator felt drained, as if after an epileptic convulsion.

The entire incident could have been something else. He would not now be surprised if they were to tell him that his inquiry was as far from the truth as a biography of the pope, a file on a bank loan or the life story of a trafficked woman from the former East, recorded in desolate police offices near airports.

"I will ask one more question," he said gently. "Let it be the last. I want to know if, as you drove towards the airport, you heard a strange noise, which you might at first have taken to be an engine fault, but was in fact something else. A noise quite unexpected on a motorway, like a galloping horse chasing you all."

He stood up without waiting for the answer.

9

The researcher now felt relief rather than despair at having abandoned any attempt to describe the final week.

His conclusion was that not only the final moments in the taxi but the entire last week were impossible to describe. He felt no guilt at cutting his story short. On the contrary, he felt it would have been wrong to continue.

From every great secret, hints occasionally leak out. It is probably once in seven, ten or seventy millennia that something escapes from that appalling repository where the gods store their superior knowledge that is forbidden to humankind. And in that moment, something that would normally take centuries to be discovered is suddenly revealed to the unseeing human eye, as when the wind accidentally lifts a veil.

In that moment of time, these four, that is, the two passengers, the driver and the mirror, apparently found themselves in an impossible conjunction.

Something impossible happened, the driver had said. In other words, something that was beyond their understanding. It was like a story of souls whose bodies are absent. It was this dissociation of body and soul that evidently led to their sense of disorientation and intoxicating liberation, the uncoupling of form and essence.

The file of the inquiry showed that Rovena and Besfort had mentioned this dissociation several times. They had also probably come to regret it.

He recalled now those few ideas, like rare diamonds, that he had exchanged with the pianist about Besfort's final dream.

What was Besfort looking for in the tomb–motel? They agreed that he was looking for Rovena. Murdered, according to Lulu Blumb; disfigured, according to himself. Or perhaps something similar, which millions of men search for: the second nature of the woman they love.

For hours he imagined Besfort in front of this plaster structure, waiting for the original Rovena, then in the taxi, beside her fugitive form, experiencing something impossible for anybody in this world.

10

It was a silent Sunday noon when Liza Blumberg phoned again after a long interval. Unlike on previous occasions, her voice was warm and somnolent.

"I'm calling to tell you that I withdraw my suggestion that Besfort murdered my friend Rovena."

"Why?" he replied. "You were so certain . . ."

"And now I am certain of the opposite."

"I see," he said after a silence.

He waited for Lulu to say something more, or to hang up.

"Rovena is alive," she went on. "Only she's changed her hair colour and now she's called Anevor."

Late that afternoon, Lulu Blumb arrived to recount what had happened the night before.

She had been playing the piano in the late-night bar, the very place where the two women had first met years before. It was the same bar and the same time, just before midnight, and she was feeling sick at heart, when Rovena appeared before her.

Lulu sensed her presence as soon as she came through the door, but an indistinct fear that she might change her mind and turn back would not allow her to lift her head from the piano keyboard.

The woman who had entered made her way slowly among the chairs and sat down in the same place as on that fateful evening long ago. She had dyed her hair blonde, to preserve her anonymity, as Lulu realised later. But she walked in the same way, and her eyes, which once you had seen you could never forget, had not changed.

Then they stared at each other, as they had done that first time, but some invisible impediment made Lulu respect the newcomer's wish not to be recognised.

Meanwhile, her fingers, which had played so naturally on the body of the woman she loved, conveyed to the keyboard all her grief at Rovena's absence, her emotion at finding her again, her desire and its impediment.

As she finished, exhausted, her head bent, she listened to the whispers of "Bravo!" and waited for her to join her admirers by the piano as she had done before.

She did come, last in line, pale with emotion.

Rovena, my darling, Liza Blumberg cried to herself. But the other woman uttered a different name.

But still she repeated what she had said long ago, and, shortly before the bar closed, the couple found themselves once more in the pianist's car.

They kissed for a long time in silence. But each time Liza whispered the name Rovena, she failed to respond. They went on kissing and tears moistened the cheeks of both, but it was only in bed after midnight when they were on the verge of sleep that Liza finally said, "You are Rovena. Why are you hiding it?" And the other woman replied, "You're confusing me with someone else." After a silence she said it again, "You're confusing me with someone else," and added, "but what does it matter?"

Really, what does it matter? thought Lulu Blumb. It was the same love, only in a different shape.

"Did you say a name?" the young woman said. "Did you say the name Rovena?" If she liked it so much, she could use an anagram, as people liked to do these days: Anevor.

Anevor, repeated Lulu Blumb to herself. Like the name of a witch in ancient times. You can dye your hair, change your passport and try a thousand tricks, but nothing in the world will persuade me that you are not Rovena.

As she stroked her chest, she found the scar left by the bullet of his revolver in that scary Albanian motel. She kissed it gently without saying a word.

She had so many questions. How had she managed to escape Besfort? How had she duped him?

With this thought she fell asleep. When she woke next morning Rovena had gone. Lulu would have taken her visit for a dream, but for the note left on the piano:

"I didn't want to wake you. Thank you for this miracle. Your Anevor."

"And that was all," said Liza in a tired voice, after a silence, before she stood up to leave.

As so often before, the investigator's gaze was caught by the last photograph, which showed Rovena's dark hair and her delicate arm extended across Besfort's chest, stretching towards the knot of his tie, as if trying to undo it at the last moment and help release his troubled spirit.

From the window, the researcher watched the woman reach the other side of the crossroads. A distant peal of thunder made him shake his head, but he could not say why, or to whom this negative was directed.

So Lulu Blumb was gone too. She had let him go quietly, as she had done with so many things in this world, and perhaps that distant reverberation was her kind of farewell.

Now he would be left by himself as before, alone with the riddle of the two strangers that nobody had asked him to solve.

I I

The researcher had imagined it before, and would do so hundreds of times before his life's end: the painful progress of the taxi through the traffic on that blustery morning of 17 May, the rain beating against the windows, the long stationary lines, the names of firms and distant cities written on trucks in all the languages of Europe. Dortmund, Euromobil, Hannover, Elsinore, Paradise Travel, The Hague. These names, and their low voices, "What's this doomsday scenario, we're going to miss the plane." – all these things added to their anxiety.

Of course it is late. They want to turn back, even if they do not say so. On both sides, the trap is closing.

"Let's go back, darling."

"We can't."

They talk in low voices, not knowing if the other can hear. There's absolutely no way back. The rear-view mirror reflects the eyes of one and then the other. The traffic moves a little. Later it stalls again. Perhaps they'll hold the plane. Frankfurt

Intercontinental, Vienna, Monaco–Hermitage, Kronprinz. Her mind reels. But we've stayed in these hotels. (Where we were happy, she whispers fearfully.) Why have they suddenly turned against us? Loreley, Schlosshotel-Lerbach, Excelsior Ernst, Biarritz. He tries to hold her tight.

"Don't be scared, darling. I think the traffic's easing. Perhaps the plane will wait." He puts his arm around her, but the gesture seems distant, as if long-forgotten.

"What are those black oxen?" she says. "That's all we need."

He makes no reply, but mutters something about prison doors. He hopes they'll find them still open, before the sun sets. She is scared again. She wants to ask: where did we go wrong? He tries to draw her close.

"What are you doing? You're strangling me."

The taxi speeds forward. The driver's eyes, as if already caught by something, freeze on the glass of the mirror. Light pours in from both sides, but it is too bright, pitiless. She lays her head against his shoulder. The taxi begins to shake. There is an alien presence inside, prepotent, heedless, with its own powers and menacing laws. What's happening? Where are we going wrong? Their lips come still closer. We mustn't. We can't. There are prohibitive powers and orders everywhere. He says something inaudible. From the movement of his lips, it is a name, but someone else's, not hers. He repeats it, but again, as in his plaster dream, it cannot be heard. He pleads for the return of the woman he has killed with his own hands. Please come back, be again what you were. But she cannot. No way. Whole minutes, years, centuries pass until there is a great crack, and from out of the encasing plaster the name finally resounds: Eurydice. The tremors suddenly cease. As if the taxi has left the earth. The doors spring open and seem to give the car wings. And so transformed, it flies through the sky, unless it never was a taxi, but something else, and they had failed to notice. But it is too late now. There is no remedy.

Rovena and Besfort Y. are no longer . . . Anevor . . .

Dlrow siht ni regnol on era Y. trofseB dna anevoR . . .

12

More and more often he fell into a drowsy state, from which only the prospect of writing his own will could rouse him. Before drafting it he waited for a final answer from the European Road Safety Institute. Its reply came after a long delay. The Institute accepted his condition. He would deliver to them the results of his inquiry in exchange for the taxi's rear-view mirror.

In the offices which he visited, they looked at him in surprise, and even with a kind of pity, as if he were sick. At the waste disposal site, he met with a similar reception. It took a long time to find the mirror; he could hardly believe his eyes when at last they handed it to him.

It was not easy to prepare his will. In the course of writing it, he discovered that there was an infinite universe of testaments. Down the ages, history had recorded the most diverse kinds. Testaments had been left in the form of poisons, antique tragedies, storks' nests, appeals by national minorities or metro projects. The material attachments appended to them were no less surprising, ranging from revolvers and condoms, to oil pipes and the devil knew what. The taxi's rear-view mirror, buried with the man who had been so preoccupied with it in life, was the first such object of its kind.

He handed over the text of his will for translation into Latin and then into the principal languages of the European Union. He spent weeks sending it to every possible institution he could find on the internet: archaeological institutes, psycho-mystical research units, university departments of geochemistry. A huge and deadly bunker in the United States. Finally, the World Probate Institute.

While dealing with all this, he heard vague pieces of news, some about the long-standing question of whether Besfort Y. had murdered his girlfriend or not. Opinions were as divided as ever. Now there was a third view, that Besfort had indeed committed a murder, but it was impossible to ascertain at what time. In this case the allegation of murder had to be withdrawn, unless it could be shown to have been committed in another dimension in which actions do not take place in time, because time does not exist.

As expected, there were also rumours that Rovena St. (as time passed, some interpreted St. as an abbreviation of "Saint") was still alive. It was said that Besfort Y. too had been seen, hurrying across a road junction with the collar of his overcoat raised in order not to be recognised. He was even sighted in Tirana, sitting on a sofa after dinner, persuading a young woman to take a trip with him round Europe.

Absorbed in his will, he tried to forget all these things. He returned to the text every day. He would correct words here and there, or remove and replace them, but without altering the essential content.

His will essentially provided for the reopening of his grave, in which, inside his lead coffin, the famous mirror would be buried beside his body.

First, he set a date for his exhumation thirty years hence. Later, he changed this to one hundred, only to erase this and write one thousand years.

He spent what life remained to him imagining what the diggers would find when they opened his grave. He firmly believed that mirrors, into which women looked as they beautified themselves before they were kissed, or murdered, absorbed something of the images they reflected. But nobody in this scornful world had thought of taking an interest in any of this.

He hoped that what happened in the taxi carrying two lovers to an airport, one thousand years ago, would leave some trace, however slight, on the surface of the glass.

There were days when he thought he discerned the outline of this mystery, as if through mist, but there were others when it seemed that the mirror, even after lying for a thousand years next to his skull, opaquely reflected nothing but the infinite void.

Tirana, Mali i Robit, Paris
Winter, 2003–2004